PRAISE FOR
THE MYSTERY OF THE RADCLIFFE RIDDLE

"*The Mystery of the Radcliffe Riddle* is a fantastic mix of mystery, history, friendship, and heart. Taryn Souders is masterful at weaving clues and suspense to create a riveting story that you won't want to put down!"

—Christina Diaz Gonzalez, Edgar Award-winning author of *Concealed*

"A clever mystery with a big heart."

—Lindsay Currie, author of *Scritch Scratch*

PRAISE FOR
COOP KNOWS THE SCOOP
AN EDGAR AWARD NOMINEE FOR BEST JUVENILE MYSTERY

"An engrossing, good-humored page-turner."

—*Kirkus Reviews*

"Will have readers guessing until the truth comes out."

—*Publishers Weekly*

"Lovers of mysteries are sure to appreciate the uniqueness of this piece."

—*The Bulletin of the Center for Children's Books*

PRAISE FOR
HOW TO (ALMOST) RUIN YOUR SUMMER

"As fun as the book's description sounds."

—*Cracking the Cover*

"An entertaining and lighthearted choice..."

—*School Library Journal*

ALSO BY TARYN SOUDERS

Coop Knows the Scoop

How to (Almost) Ruin Your Summer

THE MYSTERY OF THE
RADCLIFFE RIDDLE

THE MYSTERY OF THE RADCLIFFE RIDDLE

TARYN SOUDERS

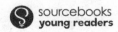
sourcebooks
young readers

Published by Sourcebooks Young Readers, an imprint of Sourcebooks
P.O. Box 4410, Naperville, Illinois 60567–4410
(630) 961-3900
sourcebooks.com

Cataloging-in-Publication Data is on file with the Library of Congress.

This product conforms to all applicable CPSC and CPSIA standards.

Source of Production: Marquis Book Printing, Montreal, QC, Canada
Date of Production: April 2024
Run Number: 5041112

Printed and Bound in Canada.
MBP 10 9 8 7 6 5 4 3

To treasure hunters and detectives everywhere

... and to Uncle Dan, for where your treasure is,

there will your heart be also.

CHAPTER 1

"EUDORA KLINCH DIED." I lowered myself onto the warped boards of the dock, next to Thad, and set *The Gifton Gazette* between us.

My feet dangled above the water for an instant, then I thought better of it and removed my sneakers. I'd found them in the church donation box last week, and while they were in decent enough shape, the fit was a bit loose, and I didn't care to lose one or both to Chapman's Pond.

The murky water didn't seem to bother Ophelia much. The squirrel-chasing mutt who belonged to no one in Gifton, but was looked after by nearly everyone, barreled down the dock and leapt into the pond.

"Why are you reading the obituaries, Grady?" Thad asked. "It's creepy."

"I've got nothing else to read." I swung my feet back and forth. "It's Sunday. The library's closed and I've read everything I checked out last week." And it wasn't like I could buy books when I ran out of something to read.

Ophelia swam to shore and disappeared into the woods chasing a squirrel.

Thad yanked a narrow bag of shelled sunflower seeds from his back pocket and poured a few into his hand. "Want some?"

"No thanks." I pushed my hair away from my eyes. I needed a haircut, but they cost money, and I wasn't about to trust Thad with a pair of scissors.

He flipped open his sketchbook and began another floor plan. If Thad wasn't drawing houses, he was reading about them, or about architects. It was all part of his plan to become a world-famous architect himself. "I wonder if Kooky's ghost is digging up flowers for her heavenly mansion."

Eudora Klinch had earned her nickname—Kooky—due to the fact she had hauled a shovel with her wherever she went, and she'd dug more holes around town than a gopher on caffeine. Rumor had it, ages ago her ancestors buried something valuable somewhere in Gifton, but no one had ever found any treasure, not even Kooky Klinch.

Every so often she'd dig up some poor soul's graveside flowers, claiming to have finally found the long-lost treasure, and then take them back to her house for replanting. Deputy Oringderff had long since given up talking to her about it. Said she saw no point in upsetting her, since it was obvious Miss Eudora's corn bread wasn't quite cooked all the way through.

Thankfully, she'd never taken the flowers from Mama's grave. Dad would've had a fit. Me too.

At least that's *one* thing we'd have agreed on.

Without Mama in between us, it had become so obvious Dad and I were on opposite sides in almost everything. If hope was a thing with feathers—like that Emily Dickinson poem that had been Mama's favorite—mine had a broken wing. Or maybe I just had the wrong kind of bird. I figured Emily was saying hope was like a bird in her chest that sang no matter what. It sounded like maybe she had a sweet canary or something cheerful inside her.

But not me.

I had an annoying mockingbird, poking fun at my attempt to get along with Dad.

And I was pretty sure *he* had a vulture.

What I really wanted was Emily Dickinson's canary.

"What are y'all doing?" Clemmie's voice called from behind.

Thad jumped and accidentally sideswiped the package of sunflower seeds right into the pond. "Frank Lloyd Wright! Why are you scaring me like that?"

Thad's idea of swearing was to spew architects' names. At

least I'd heard of *this* one. Clemmie wasn't allowed to swear, but she usually didn't let that stop her.

I glanced over my right shoulder, shielding my eyes from the afternoon sun. Clemmie, in a brown tank a shade lighter than her skin, sauntered down the dock toward us with a swagger that radiated self-confidence. "You're going to turn into a boiled lobster." Her voice dragged its way through the soupy air and made its way to my ears.

I knew she wasn't talking to me. Along with inheriting Mama's Welsh green eyes and dark hair, I also had her olive skin, and it took a lot for me to be mistaken for a boiled lobster.

"Like you never burn?" Thad said.

"I don't, doofus. I just get darker." She flipped a handful of braids over her shoulder. "And before you ask, yes, Black people can also get freckles."

"No fair," he muttered. Thad was so white he could blend in with potato salad. Redheads are pale, but he took it to a whole new level. "And you made me drop my snack." He stared mournfully at his floating bag of sunflower seeds. He reached down and pulled it out before it could sink to the bottom. Thad was drawn to food the same way moths are drawn to light. His stomach and love of architecture were his two main purposes for waking up. And despite the fact he ate all the time, a strong wind could probably blow him over.

"Guess what?" Clemmie said, wiggling in between us and bringing the scent of coconut lotion with her. She smelled loads better than Thad or me. "I won our ever-so-official Battle of the Battles."

A couple weeks back before school ended, our history teacher, Mrs. Maragos, had crammed in a last-minute lesson about a bit of a kerfuffle during Georgia's colonial history, the War of Jenkins's Ear. Some British guy got his ear cut off by some Spanish guy and eight years of war followed. Even though a good chunk of the fighting happened in the Caribbean, parts of it took place near Gifton—stuff like militia raids and skirmishes.

After that history lesson, Clemmie, Thad, and I tried to see who could find the dumbest reason to start a war. All we'd discovered so far were that noble causes like freedom and liberty were few and far between, but dumb reasons were as common as mosquitoes on a summer night.

"What makes you think *you're* the winner?" Thad asked.

Clementine Powell and Thaddeus Carlton were as different as cherries and cheese, but you'd be hard-pressed to find a closer pair of friends. Somehow, they made it work.

Unlike Dad and me.

Clemmie poked him in the chest. "I don't think. I *know*. Ever hear about the War of the Golden Stool?"

Thad scowled. "The what?"

"I didn't think so." Clemmie grinned and glanced down at his sketchbook. "Nice house, by the way."

"Can't it wait?" I wiped away a bead of sweat. "I was about to tell him about Eudora Klinch."

"She's not going anywhere. Hold on."

"But—"

Clemmie erased my protest with a wave of her hand. "Later, Grady."

I groaned. Arguing with her was useless. She was the shortest of the three of us, but tough as a pine knot when she had her mind set on something.

"Look here." She leaned toward me and pulled a folded piece of paper from her back pocket. "Some British diplomat back in 1900—and why does it always seem to be the British?—demanded to sit on a stool that was considered sacred to the Ashanti people—they're in Africa—and *bam*, war broke out." She thrust the paper toward Thad. "Read it. People died."

Thad folded the sheet in half and fanned his face.

"Speaking of people who died," I said, "let's get back to Eudora Klinch."

Clemmie rested back on her hands and crossed her ankles. "Is it true she was rich?"

Thad stopped fanning. "And cats! Didn't she have a million

of them? I remember one bit Ernie's big toe last year. Held on tight too, until Ernie fed it one of his chicken nuggets."

Hard to blame the cat. Ernie Dixon was practically feral himself and smelled like chicken nuggets because that's all he ever ate. His folks weren't around much, and, according to him, his pet turtle Shelldon didn't mind the smell and would even eat an occasional chunk of chicken himself.

I rolled my eyes. "The obituary doesn't mention money or cats. It'd be in bad taste." I swiped the fan from Thad and handed him the newspaper. "Here, look."

He flapped it open and read aloud.

> "The rather eccentric Eudora Klinch surely went on to receive her heavenly reward last Thursday at the overripe age of 98. She lived in Gifton her whole life. She was an only child and never married. Miss Klench often won Yard of the Month for the beautiful flowers in her front lawn."

Clemmie shook her head. "The mayor can't even get her name right."

Mayor Shore ran *The Gifton Gazette*. He was reporter, editor in chief, and obit writer. The good man hadn't developed a habit of proofreading any better than he developed photographs. The weekly newspaper was simply Deputy Oringderff's police report sprinkled with blurry pictures, expired coupons, opinions, and typos.

Thad turned his attention back to the paper.

"A graveside service will be held this Tuesday at four o'clock. Y'all know where. Feel free to bring flowers from Eudora's front lawn—they were most likely yours to begin with anyway. Come if you have nothing else going on. Charlie Waddell, do not bring a date this time."

I swatted away a mosquito. "I think we should go."
Thad pulled the *Gazette* down. "Why?"
"Keep reading."

"Reception provided by Gifton Cooking Society to follow immediately after. Please RSVP to Miss Ida Rose Cloyd who will be heading up the somber affair."

If anything good or bad happened in town, Ida Rose was guaranteed to be present and handing out food.

"On second thought, we *should* pay our respects." Thad handed back the newspaper.

Clemmie smacked her lips. "I hope she brings cake."

"I want her fried chicken," Thad said.

"Are you serious? I'm definitely not eating her fried chicken," Clemmie said. "If she eats that on a regular basis, her funeral will probably be next."

Ida Rose turned out fried chicken so greasy the undertaker probably could've tossed a couple pieces into Eudora Klinch's coffin ahead of time and just let her glide through the Pearly Gates.

~~~

But the following week we learned that Clemmie, for all her many talents, was no fortune teller. Ida Rose was not the next Gifton resident to kick the bucket.

CHAPTER 2

ON THURSDAY, TWO DAYS after the late, unlamented Miss Eudora Klinch was laid to rest, Dad and I sat in our usual spot at Charlie's Diner, the booth closest to the front door. Dad and Charlie Waddell had struck a bargain a couple years back: carpentry work for hotcakes. No one knew if the deal had an end date, but either Charlie liked having a handyman on retainer—ready to fix his broken tables or build flower boxes for the front walk or do whatever else needed doing—or he enjoyed sharing his hotcakes. Whichever way, I didn't mind one bit because otherwise Dad and I would never eat out.

And I like eating out. I like being in the diner and feeling like a normal guy, like everyone else in town. The only difference was everyone else in town chitchatted at their table. Not Dad and me. We ate in near silence, answering the occasional question with one- or two-word responses, or even a grunt. Pretty much like we'd done for the last couple years.

I looked around. All the regulars were there. In the far corner, Roland Spears sat visiting with Ida Rose. Charlie stood behind the long counter pouring coffee into Badger Paulin's cup for the fourth time. If drinking coffee was a crime, Badger was a repeat offender. But despite his love of caffeine and being named after a surly animal, Badger Paulin was as calm as a southern breeze...unless he was driving in the Tipton County Lawn Mower Derby, and then all bets were off. A few stools down, Badger's older sister, Winifred, sat head-to-head with Arlene McGinter at the counter.

Miss Arlene's tight silver coils barely moved as her head bobbed in agreement with whatever Winifred had just said. Since there were hardly any wrinkles on Miss Arlene's dark skin, her silver hair and walking cane were the only things that hinted at the fact she was in her eighties.

Arliss, her husband, sat next to her and fiddled with his hearing aid, which hadn't worked properly for quite some time. A year ago, he'd simply taken to shouting at everyone, which was a bit backward since the rest of us could all hear fine.

Next to him was the mayor's wife, Muggie, whose real name no one remembered. She ran the Gifton Museum on the second floor of the courthouse library. She considered gossip a valid historical source. She leaned past Arliss, listening to Winifred and Arlene, all the while fiddling with her necklace. You'd have a better chance seeing Muggie without shoes on her feet than without her fake pearls.

Muggie came from "old money," but her uncle Harold had stolen most of it ages ago and then ran off to the Marshall Islands to avoid being caught by the police. Supposedly any remaining real jewelry was sold and replaced with knockoffs. I guess Muggie's family hoped their secret would be safe, but they didn't take Winifred Paulin into account. Secrets poured out of her like water from a fountain.

She came by her gift of gab honestly though, with well over three hundred years of talkative genetics pumping through her system. Dad blamed it on the fact she hailed from a long line of preachers, starting with the Reverend Joseph Stone way back when Gifton was founded. It was no small wonder Winifred could talk the ears off an elephant.

Clemmie said Winifred would no more lay a bit of gossip to rest than would let her curls turn gray. She was the only seventy-year-old I knew with maroon hair.

Charlie spoke and made me forget about Winifred's maroon hair. "Well now, *he* certainly ain't your typical day-tripper." He stood by the front door holding an empty pot of coffee after wandering around and giving refills.

The room fell silent as we all turned toward the diner's large front windows.

But the silence only lasted for an instant.

Then the scraping of chairs and the stampeding of feet filled the air. Plates abandoned, people sitting at the counter and the far tables scurried to booths near the windows and squeezed in with those of us already seated. Badger slipped in next to me and tried to press his face against the glass. Muggie wedged herself next to Badger. Good thing they built the foundation of Charlie's Diner on a concrete slab, because if his restaurant rested on cinder blocks like our mobile home, the whole place would've tipped over on its side.

I elbowed Badger. "You're squishing me."

A man with a unibrow that looked like a big ol' hairy caterpillar was crawling across his face stood on the other side of Maple Street. He scowled as he glanced back and forth from a paper in his hand to the diner. His fancy suit-and-tie getup separated him from the average Joe who occasionally came to Gifton for boring antique shopping.

"He's headed this way!" Muggie called. "Act natural!"

A mad scramble back to seats and stools ensued, and by the time the man walked through the door, everyone was talking like it was just another normal day. Jessie Mae Stevens swished around the tables topping off coffee cups, and the clinking of silverware against plates filled the air.

"Morning," Charlie said loudly, wiping down the counter. "Can I help you?"

The man cleared his throat. "I'm Myron Burns of Burns, Burns, & Burns."

Badger swiveled on his stool. "What is that? A boy band? What kind of music do y'all sing?"

Some people, like Arliss, are hard of hearing. Not Badger. People say he's hard of thinking, and chances are, they're right.

Mr. Burns grimaced. "It's a law firm. I'm an attorney."

"Well, I'll be." Badger swiped some crumbs off the stool next to him and gestured toward it. "Have a seat."

Mr. Burns shifted the briefcase to his other hand and eyed the crowded diner. "I'm not here to eat."

"This is an odd place to be if you're not wanting to eat." Badger held his mug out to Charlie for another refill.

"I'm looking for a Mr. Kevin Judd," the man said, turning and scanning the room once more. "A boy near his house told me I'd find him here."

A quiet curse escaped Dad's lips. He set his fork down.

I wondered if one of the people Dad owed money to had sent the lawyer. Does the electric company sue you if you're a couple months late? It wasn't Dad's fault he was always behind on bills. Mama had lingered in a coma for seven weeks before passing. Bills of all sorts had piled up faster than the cars had on the interstate the day of her accident.

Winifred slid off her stool, and busybodied herself over to where he stood. "Who?"

"Kevin Judd," Mr. Burns repeated slowly, eyeballing her maroon hair with what might've been curiosity, but was most likely suspicion.

Badger took a sip of coffee. "I think she means who told you?"

"How should I know?" Mr. Burns scoffed. "He had red hair that stuck up in at least ten different directions and was eating. There was a dog too—who, I'm fairly certain, had a squirrel in its mouth."

"Ah! That'd be Ophelia," Badger said.

Mr. Burns's brow crinkled in confusion. "I could've sworn he was a boy."

Dad slid a hand over his face and pushed out of the booth, probably to pause the conversation before it went anymore sideways. "The boy is Thad. The dog is Ophelia. The squirrel's been dead for a while." He sighed. "I'm Kevin Judd." He gestured toward our table. "This is my son, Grady. Care to join us?"

I gave a small wave.

Mr. Burns glanced over both his shoulders. "I don't normally handle legal matters in such a public setting. Is there somewhere private we can talk?"

"Not in this town," Dad muttered, sliding back into the booth. "You can't clean out a cat box without it being front-page news. They'll discover it soon enough. Somehow, some way—never fails."

Mr. Burns shrugged and dragged a chair up to our table as everyone in the diner pretended to return to their conversations, but I wasn't fooled. Each person had one ear listening in our direction.

Dad cleared his throat and leaned toward Mr. Burns. He lowered his voice. "If this is about our late mortgage payment, I can—"

Mr. Burns held up a hand. "It isn't." He sat, resting his brief-case on his lap. "I made repeated phone calls, but—"

"We haven't had a phone for a few months now," I said faintly.

"Clearly." Mr. Burns murmured.

Dad had a cell for his business, but it was prepaid and used sparingly. When we needed to call someone, Dad would send me through the woods to Thad's house. The Carltons never commented, but my face still burned with embarrassment each time.

"Therefore," Mr. Burns continued, "I drove here to deliver the news and to have you sign the necessary papers."

Dad folded his hands on the table. "What news?"

"Speak up!" Arliss tapped his hearing aid and turned to Miss Arlene. "Is this thing on?"

Excitement overcame Winifred like a tent revival with everyone swaying, singing, and praising the good Lord. Unable to control herself, she came and stood behind Mr. Burns, trembling with anticipation. Others leaned in toward our booth.

Mr. Burns glanced up at her and then cleared his throat. "News that your late relative, Miss Eudora Klinch of Gifton, Georgia, left you something in her will."

CHAPTER 3

A GASP FLEW FROM Winifred's mouth. "Oh my!"

"We're related?" I squawked.

The diner exploded in a buffet of chatter.

Badger spewed coffee into his mug. "Y'all kin to Kooky Klinch?"

Arliss tugged on Miss Arlene's arm. "What did he say about a wrench?"

Dad faced Mr. Burns. "You have the wrong family. We weren't related to Eudora. We've lived in Gifton our whole lives, and I think we'd know if we had relatives here."

"That's right." Winifred tapped him on the shoulder. "Everybody knows everyone's history here. You can't hide a relation any more than you can hide that unibrow of yours."

Mr. Burns scowled at Winifred, his unibrow veeing down into a frown. "Well, clearly neither *you* nor Mr. Judd knew his son, Grady, was related to Miss Klinch. He is Eudora's first cousin twice removed." He faced me. "Miss Klinch didn't know she was related to you any more than you knew you were related to her. She wrote in her will that if we could find a relative then she had something for them."

"Well, I know *my* family history," Winifred said. "All the way from the blessed Reverend Joseph Stone to—"

Charlie cut her off. "Just because *you're* always jabbering on about how you come from such a long line of preachers doesn't mean *we all* have our family tree memorized. I wouldn't know a first cousin twice removed if one walked through that front door."

"*Pshaw.*" She batted aside his response as we all turned and stared at the front door just in case an unknown relative of Charlie's did walk in.

Mr. Burns pulled a pair of glasses from his suitcoat pocket, along with a piece of paper that looked like a list of names. He put the glasses on and tapped the first name on the list. "You see, Thomas Klinch—"

"Eudora's grandaddy," Winifred said.

"Exactly," Mr. Burns said. "He went out west to look for work. After he died—"

"He was trying to catch a free ride on a train," Winifred said. "Fell off and was run over. Such a tragedy and there was Minerva left all alone with five children to feed. Good hardworking family. The oldest children took odd jobs. Did all they could to help their mama."

"Winifred, how would you know that?" Badger asked. "I know you ain't that old."

She gave Badger a withering look. "Eudora knew about her own grandaddy and how he died. Naturally, we talked." She raised her chin. "That's how I know.'"

"The two youngest were shipped off to families up north," continued Mr. Burns, referring to the list. "They were meant to be reunited at some point, but Minerva died of tuberculosis before her two young ones ever returned home. Judith, the youngest, married a man name Henry Gregory and they lived in Boston."

Dad nodded. "I recognize the name Henry Gregory. He was my wife's grandfather. He and his wife both died before I met Gretchen. I had no idea her grandmother was from Gifton. What are the odds?"

Muggie elbowed her way closer to our booth. "But what about all those other kids? Winifred said Thomas Klinch had five children, and Winifred is never wrong."

Mr. Burns shook his head. "Are you an attorney arguing against this inheritance? Believe me"—he waved the list of names in the air—"we have traced this family tree carefully. Would you like me to tell you when each of the other relatives died?" His tone of voice said there was no way he was going to spend any time explaining to the diner about how all Eudora's relatives—my relatives—had died. Which was too bad because I would have liked to hear it. I didn't know much about my mom's family.

Dad looked thunderstruck. "Unbelievable. I met my Gretchen in Atlanta—she was working for Delta when I was doing construction on the airport." He looked at Roland Spears as if he needed reassurance that he was remembering things correctly.

Roland nodded. "That's right. Bo Forester hired us both for that project. Big job."

"And you come home with a wife you brought back from parts unknown," Winifred said. "But we all forgave you since she was such a sugar. And here we find out she's Gifton folk all along. No wonder she was as nice as a tall glass of sweet tea."

Mr. Burns took more folded papers from his jacket pocket. "Our firm did impeccable research into Eudora Klinch's family line. Here's the official genealogy." He slid the information across to Dad. "It's all right there."

Dad gave the long document a quick look, slid it over to me, then looked at the lawyer with a glint of hope in his eyes. "You say she left us something?"

Mr. Burns placed his briefcase on the table.

I grabbed the leather bracelet on my wrist, the one Clemmie had made for me at summer camp the year before, and twisted it back and forth. A nervous habit.

"I mean, no matter how much—even a small amount will help." Dad cracked his knuckles. *His* nervous habit. Something I'd noticed he'd been doing more and more.

The latches on Mr. Burns's briefcase opened with a double click.

My mouth felt dry and gritty like a sandstorm had blown across my throat. I took a gulp of water, but it didn't help.

"We're grateful for whatever she left," Dad said. "There's truck repairs, house repairs, mountains of bills, you name it. It's hard getting to and from work. Evrol breaks down every other week." Babbling seemed to be another one of Dad's nervous habits. But at least he appeared younger than he had just minutes ago.

Mr. Burns stared at him. "Evrol?"

He nodded. "My truck."

Years of rust, chipped paint, and the way Dad drove in reverse had either dissolved, dented, or scraped off several of the letters spelling out CHEVROLET on the back, leaving behind only E V R O L.

Mr. Burns lifted the briefcase lid.

My heart knocked against my rib cage harder...and then faster.

Hearing I was related to the town eccentric made me

twitch. But what made me even twitchier was wondering if Clemmie was right about her being rich. Maybe Mr. Burns had a gold bar in his case. Or stacks of bills? Or stock certificates worth millions?

I swallowed. We could own a real truck. A real house. At the moment, Dad and I lived in a run-down mobile home on the outskirts of Gifton that we moved into after Mama died. It sat on about five acres of land overrun with trees, but the property had a workshop, so Dad had figured it was a good deal.

In other words, it was all we could afford.

But now I bet we'd take down the FOR SALE sign Dad had nailed to the fence on County Road 1A a couple months ago. He'd said he was just trying to sell some of the acreage, so I wasn't concerned, but I knew Dad loved the land.

And maybe we'd move into Kooky Klinch's house. It was old and the paint was faded, but it was practically a mansion. No more leaky roof when it rained. No more cold nights during winter, or sheets sticking to me in the heat of summer. We could afford air-conditioning.

Dad and I could take a vacation…like we used to when Mama was alive. He'd never go anywhere if he had a choice. He was stubborn enough to make a preacher cuss, Mama used to say. But she managed to drag him off at least once a year. She always said, "The family that plays together stays together."

Until one of them dies, that is. No amount of playing could stop death on a slick-as-snot roadway cutting through a foggy Georgia morning.

But maybe...just maybe he and I could still be a family that stayed together. Maybe with all our money problems gone, Dad and I could figure out how to get along with each other.

Maybe.

Mr. Burns pulled out a flat package wrapped in brown paper and tied with string. He slid it across the table. "Miss Klinch bequeathed this to her next of kin."

Maybe she framed the stock certificates.

Dad slid it to me. "You're the blood relative, Grady. You open it."

I swallowed and looked at Dad. "You sure you don't want to?"

He shook his head. "Go for it."

I took a deep breath. Whatever was inside this package was going to change everything. Dad and I were going to be okay. I tugged on the string. My fingers trembled as I felt for the taped edges. I tore into the package and pulled away the paper.

A framed piece of faded fabric with different kinds of stitching lay under a piece of glass.

Dad glanced down, then back up, his brow furrowed. "I–I don't understand. Cross-stitch?"

The lawyer shut his briefcase. "I believe the technical term is 'sampler.'"

I leaned forward for a closer glimpse, hoping to see that it was sewn with golden thread or even silver.

Nothing glittered in the sunlight.

I flipped it over. Maybe there was money or a check taped to the back. Kind of like how I used to get with birthday cards.

Nope.

I turned it back to the front. It looked kind of like the cross-stitch hanging in Dad's room. Mama once told me she'd made it right after they were married and patterned it after one from the Civil War she'd seen in an antique store. My dreams of a new house, truck, and vacation shredded and crumbled into dust, like the frayed edges of the rotting cloth in front of Dad.

"A sampler, you said?" Arlene McGinter prodded her way through the crowd with her cane and tapped Mr. Burns's chair. "Scoot over, young man. Let me have a look."

Miss Arlene possessed a quiet strength that people noticed. Mr. Burns huffed but shifted to the side and made room.

Arliss and Arlene McGinter owned the Music Box, the local antique shop. The first thing Arliss ever sold was a threadbare cymbal-playing monkey sitting on top of a music box. He was so proud of his sale that he and his wife had named their store after it.

Miss Arlene peered at the framed piece. "Hmmm…I doubt the needlework has much value, but even without my glasses I can tell the frame is quite old." Her fingers gently brushed the carved wood and she hummed. "Gilded too. Lovely."

"You call that lovely?" Charlie blanched. "That frame's uglier than sin."

He wasn't wrong. Not only was it ugly, but it was flat-out creepy. A carved, grinning cherub face decorated each corner.

Miss Arlene ignored Charlie and patted Dad's hand. "Think on it for a couple days, Kevin. If you don't want it, bring it to the Music Box. I know a collector in Savannah, and the whole kit and caboodle can be sold for about $75 and shipped lickety-split." She slid out of the booth and made her way back through the crowd.

Seventy-five dollars? Dad couldn't even buy Evrol one new tire, let alone four, for that paltry amount.

"What about Kooky's house?" Badger called.

"Miss Klinch left *that*, plus its contents, to her cats," said Mr. Burns.

Dad's shoulders dropped. "Her cats?" His voice came out in a squeak barely noticeable over the laughter that exploded in the diner.

"The Tipton County Cat Society to be exact," Mr. Burns said. "Along with everything in her savings account." He grunted. "She got a bit…eccentric in her old age."

Dad looked like someone had just taken away Christmas. I felt the same way.

"The rest of her estate—which consists of the contents of her safe-deposit box—goes to her next of kin," Mr. Burns said.

Dad perked up. "What was in the safe-deposit box?"

"The sampler was, along with this sealed envelope." Mr. Burns reached into his suit pocket and handed an envelope to Dad. "She also left you a half-full bag of cat food." He took his glasses off and wiped them with a napkin before tucking them back into his coat pocket. "Obviously that wasn't in the bank box. It's been sitting in my office since her passing."

"A bag of—" Dad ran his hand down his face. "We don't even own a cat."

Chuckles rippled throughout the crowd.

Dad slid his thumb under the seal. Maybe *this* would be money. Or stock certificates. Or something. He peered inside the envelope, then pulled out a narrow piece of paper. Part of a Three Musketeers wrapper stuck to the front. He peeled off the candy wrapper. "A Piggly Wiggly receipt for $100 worth of cat food," he grumbled.

"There's something written on the back," I said.

Dad flipped it over and read out loud.

To Whom It May Concern: This is no ordinary piece of needlework. It's a treasure map. Riddles

*and clues. To the victor go the riches. Don't forget
to feed the cats.*

The handwriting was squiggly, but it was signed Eudora Klinch.

"That's Kooky for you," someone said.

"Always good for a laugh," came another reply.

"Treasure! Kevin, you gonna get rich." A mischievous smile played on Badger's lips. "What I wouldn't do to get my hands on some treasure." He whistled and rubbed his hands together.

People shook their heads and, snickering, returned to their breakfasts.

Dad dropped the receipt on the table. "Eudora Klinch had more loose screws than Evrol does."

"Like I said—she'd grown eccentric." Mr. Burns pushed his chair away from the table and stood. "Maybe the boy can come get the cat food out of my car."

CHAPTER 4

DAD WAS ALREADY IN Evrol when I got there with the cat food. On the drive home, the silence inside the truck was almost as heavy as the humidity outside. I spent the time looking out my window at the giant oaks that sat back from the road. Trees were lucky. They didn't have family issues, money troubles, or loony relatives.

Dad turned down the dirt road leading to the patch of land where our mobile home sat. Both the cat food and sampler rested on the floor mat behind me, at the mercy of every pothole and dirt clod we hit. We pulled up next to the house. He turned off the sputtering engine and stared out the windshield.

"Take that thing inside, will you?" He didn't even bother to look back at the sampler. "Shove it under my bed. I don't want to see it."

"What about the cat food?"

He huffed. "It stinks and it'll attract rats. Dump it in the woods. Far away from the house." He leaned his head back and exhaled. "I think Evrol's alternator is wanting to give up the ghost. I got to run to Anaston for a part. Figure you'll probably want to hang here?"

"Yes, please," I said.

After shoving the sampler under Dad's bed, I carried the bag of cat food to the Knee Scraper. That's what Dad and I called the slab of tabby stone that lay partially hidden in the woods on the edge of our property. Someone once told me it had been the foundation to an old building, but I didn't know what kind. It was really two slabs stuck together. A smaller square-shaped one attached to a big rectangle.

Over time, trees, saplings, and brush had forced their way up through the stone cracks. In third grade, I had learned that tabby stone was a type of concrete colonists made by mixing seashells, lime, sand, and water. In sixth grade I learned if you landed on it, it hurt like thunder. Fallen leaves and moss covered much of the top, making it hard to see the uneven edges and easy to trip over—hence the name Knee Scraper.

I opened the top of the bag a little bit more and dumped the cat food on the ground. The last of the kibble tumbled out, along with a handful of mail. "Who puts mail in with cat food?" I picked up the scattered letters. "Kooky Klinch, that's who."

Two credit card offers, something from a place called Rauls Property Management, an outdated Piggly Wiggly sales flyer, and an advertisement from a pizza place over in Anaston.

I hurried back home and threw the bag into the outside trash can but hung onto the letters. Was it illegal to throw away someone else's mail? I bit my lip. I wasn't sure. The last thing Dad needed was legal problems. Plus, one letter looked like a bill, and Mr. Burns had said those would be paid by her estate or, in this case, her stupid cats.

I could go to Thad's and call the number Mr. Burns had given us back at the diner. He'd know what to do, and I could save Dad any more trouble. But first I wanted to get to the library to research samplers.

I tossed the mail on my bedroom floor, collected the books I needed to return, and then biked to the library.

Cold air blasted me when I walked through the old wooden double doors. Most libraries probably smelled like books and carpet shampoo, but not in Gifton. The wood that covered almost every inch of the former courthouse had been repeatedly polished with beeswax for over 150 years, leaving behind its honey scent and handrails so slippery they usually caused more accidents than they prevented. Even after the first floor was converted to a library and the top floor to a museum, the sweet smell remained.

I snagged an empty computer and had just finished typing *sampler* into the search bar when Clemmie tapped my shoulder. "Whatcha doing?" She pulled out the chair next to mine and leaned toward the screen. A bunch of braids fell across her arm, the beads at the tips rattling against each other. "Sampler? Like a Whitman's box of chocolates?"

I snorted and hit Enter. "Different kind of sampler."

"What's it say?" she asked.

I read from the screen. "'A piece of embroidery worked in various stitches as a specimen of skill, typically containing the alphabet, some mottoes, decorative borders, and sometimes the name of the person who embroidered it and the date. They were often used as a way to record family history and sayings of wisdom.'"

Shutting my eyes, I thought about the sampler at home. Did it have a name and date? I couldn't remember. The ancient printer took forever to boot up after I hit Print on the article. I looked around. "Is Thad here?"

She shook her head. "I stopped by his house to see if he wanted to come, but his mom said he's got a stomach bug. It's probably something he ate. He should pay more attention to expiration dates."

"Come on." I grabbed my books. "I gotta tell you about this morning. You won't believe it."

By the time we made it back to my house, I'd filled her in on most everything about Mr. Burns's visit. "So that's why I was at the library reading up on samplers," I finished.

She whistled. "Thad picked the wrong day to have food poisoning. Wait till he finds out about this."

Evrol sat parked under the giant oak near the workshop, so I knew Dad was back, but he hadn't started working on the truck yet.

"What's it look like?" Clemmie asked. "The sampler."

"It's old and the frame is super ugly." I tried to remember. "There was a house, and the alphabet, I think." I shrugged. "Some words and other stuff. I'll show you later. Dad's pretty sore about the whole thing."

"Do *you* think it's a treasure map?" she asked as we sat in the shade.

I puffed out my cheeks. "I don't know. But if *Eudora* thought it was, that would explain why she wandered around with a shovel all the time."

Clemmie snorted. "It wouldn't explain why she dug up flowers and replanted them in her yard though." That was Clemmie for you. Logical thinking was why she was the captain of the debate team at school. Her reasoning either hit you straight on or sometimes it peppered like bird shot. Either way you were toast, and I knew better than to argue with her...most of the time.

"Sometimes there's not an explanation," I said. "Sometimes things just happen."

I picked up a stick and drew silently in the dirt. Things like your mama dies but you still have your dad. Only now you don't know how to live with your dad. Or your dad doesn't know how to live with you, because the person who made it all work is no longer there.

"You thinking about you and your daddy again, Grady?"

"Don't go trying to make this something deeper than it is." I hated the fact she could see straight through me. I tossed the stick off to the side. "I was just talking. That's all. It's got nothing to do with Dad and me."

Clemmie narrowed her eyes at me. It's the kind of irritating thing she does when she's trying to read my soul. She was quiet for a minute or two, twirling one of her braids back and forth between her fingers. "I can see why your daddy would be mad. Talk about a sucker punch to the gut."

"The money would've been like winning the lotto, but a sampler is at least...interesting?"

She nudged her shoulder against mine. "I'm sorry about the cats getting everything. I really am. It sucks. And you know I'm not supposed to talk like that because it's impolite, but sometimes impolite is the only way certain things want to come out." She stood and stretched. "I better head home. You and your daddy will figure something out. Y'all always do."

CHAPTER 5

THAT NIGHT WHEN I climbed into bed, Clemmie's question still rattled around in my brain. *You thinking about you and your daddy again?*

I thought about us all the time. We worked about as well as Evrol did. Instead of Dad and me coming together after Mama's death, tension ran between us like a tightrope over Amicalola Falls. I could only hope it would get better because it couldn't get any worse.

Every so often I'd catch Dad opening the top drawer where he kept his wedding ring, staring down, and looking lost in thought. Sometimes he'd hold the ring. Maybe he was wondering what life would've been like if Mama hadn't...you know.

I'd learned when he got to a certain level of sullenness, the only company he wanted to keep was his own. We both missed her. And I longed for someone who understood me.

Maybe he did too.

∿

I shot up in bed.

It was pitch dark.

I glanced at my clock. 2:48 a.m.

A loud thud sounded somewhere. Inside the house? I couldn't tell.

"Dad?" I yell-whispered. "That you?"

I heard a shuffling sound.

No. Not Dad. The noise was outside.

The door of Dad's workshop creaked. Yanking on a shirt, I climbed out of bed, tiptoed across the dim room, and peeked around the curtain. The moon was high but just a sliver in the sky and being awful stingy with its light. I could barely make out Evrol. He sat pathetic, his hood still up from when Dad had worked on him earlier, like he was waiting for someone to take his temperature.

A shadowy figure crept from behind Evrol. I couldn't tell if it was a small bear or a person hunched over. It paused and looked in my direction. I shrunk back behind the curtain, hoping whatever or whoever it was hadn't seen me. A moment later, I peeked out again and it was gone.

But then the front doorknob rattled.

My insides turned to rock. I wanted to shout for Dad, but nothing came out.

Luckily, Ophelia was braver than me. The dog shot around the corner of the house, barking and baying and acting every bit as loony as the Shakespeare character she was named after.

My voice finally started working. "Dad!" I ran down the hall. "Dad! Wake up!"

He stumbled out of his room, wide-eyed and looking lost. "Grady? What's wrong?"

"Someone's trying to break in." My heart threatened to pound out of my chest.

Dad disappeared into his room and came out a second later with the baseball bat he kept in his closet. He flipped on the front porch light, unlocked the door, and peered out. "Wait here. I want to check the workshop and the woods."

"I'll come with—"

"No. Stay here. But if you hear me yell, grab my cell phone, and call the police. Understand?"

"Okay." My insides had turned from rock to jelly.

Dad wasn't afraid. Of course. He dashed down the steps. I followed him outside. Moths were already coming to the porch, attracted by the light. Standing on the top step, I pulled the door shut behind me.

The handle felt scratched and there were a couple small dents I hadn't noticed before.

I turned back around. Through the workshop's opened doors, I watched the beam from Dad's flashlight move methodically back and forth, then decided if he was checking things out, I should too. Maybe the would-be burglar left footprints. Or there was even a chance they had circled back around and were waiting for us to go back inside.

I hurried to my room and grabbed my flashlight. Back outside, I could see Dad checking the woods around the shed. I figured I'd look near the house. A careful sweep of the yard by the front steps offered nothing unusual. No footprints that I could see, and thankfully no strange figures lurking in the shadows. Just dirt and clumps of grass. And no trash—never any trash. Dad always said we might be dirt poor, but that didn't mean our home had to look like a dump.

I finished my search and headed back toward the front door. My flashlight beam glinted off something in the dirt near the bottom step. I picked up the small, slightly curved piece of turquoise plastic no bigger than my fingernail. It might've been left by whoever tried to break in, or it might be a bit of trash we'd missed. Just in case though, I went inside and placed it next to my lamp, then went back out to wait for Dad.

Five minutes later he came out from the woods. "Whoever it

was, they're long gone, thanks to Ophelia." He gripped a crowbar. "I found this chucked near the Knee Scraper."

"Maybe there are fingerprints on it," I said with hope.

Dad snorted. "Yeah—mine. It's our crowbar. I used it to remove some nails from a pallet earlier. And I know I left it on my workshop counter."

"So then the thief used it. Maybe *they* left prints."

Dad shrugged. "My guess is it was just some kids from Anaston being stupid on a dare."

I pointed to the marks on the door. "New scratches and dents."

He examined them. "Probably from the crowbar."

I didn't invite the fear back into my chest, but it barged in anyway. "Why would someone try to break in?"

We lived in a mobile home with peeling paint and a rusted, broken-down truck in the front yard. It was pretty obvious we didn't have anything worth stealing.

Dad squeezed my shoulder. "I'll talk to Deputy Oringderff and ask if she'll keep an extra close eye out. Sound good?"

The next day I walked to Thad's house, dying to tell him about the attempted break-in, but his mom told me he'd woken up feeling like his normal hungry self and had gone with his older brother to Atlanta to watch the Braves play and eat stadium food.

And I had no better luck at Clemmie's. Her mama had dragged her off to a health conference.

So, I ended up returning home and spending all day under a shade tree, lost in a library book. Not a bad way to spend a Friday.

Ophelia wandered into the yard at some point—came over and flopped down by me. I rubbed her ears and told her she was a good dog for chasing off whoever it was last night. She stuck around until a fresh squirrel grabbed her attention and then she disappeared.

"Grady." Dad opened the front door and leaned out. "Come here. Got an errand for you."

"Yes, sir."

I marked my place with a blade of grass. "Need me to go to the Pig?"

The Piggly Wiggly was the closest grocery store.

"No." He disappeared back inside. Whether or not he meant to slam the door, the end result was the same. Ever since Mr. Burns's visit, anything hung on a hinge was in danger.

I pushed off the ground and walked up the cinder block steps but paused at the door. In the late afternoon sun, the dents and scratches didn't look that menacing. Maybe they'd been there all along and my nerves had tricked me into thinking they were new.

The framed sampler sat in the middle of the kitchen table, next to the mail and a good-sized cardboard box. I peeked inside. Our brass lamp with flowers painted on the shade rested inside—instead of on the side table where it belonged—along with a handful of knickknacks and a few carpentry tools.

Dad walked by the rocking chair he'd made for Mama when she found out she was expecting me and set a clock radio in the box. A letter from Gifton Savings and Loan floated off the table-top in his wake. My eyes caught the INTENT TO FORECLOSE notice stamped in red across the top.

Foreclosure? Were we losing our home?

Dad wandered from room to room picking up and sometimes setting down books, picture frames, and other random things.

"Dad?"

In his bedroom, with his back to me, he said, "I need you to take that box down to the Music Box and see what you can get for it." He opened the top drawer of his dresser and his hand hovered over something, but he hesitated, and then he pushed the drawer shut.

The things in the box weren't antiques, but I knew the McGinters wouldn't let that bother them. Those were the kind of people they were. Buying modern stuff for their antique store because they knew it would help someone.

It wasn't the first time Dad had hocked items to make ends meet. Sometimes we could buy them back if the month was good and money came in, but not always.

"I've got some things in my room—"

"No." He shook his head. "I haven't sunk to the point where I hock my son's belongings."

I leaned against the doorframe. "I saw the mail. The fore—"

"We're fine." He cracked his knuckles. "I've got a big cabinet order from the Clarke family, and we'll be fine. I just need to get Evrol running so I can finish the job. Don't worry."

I nodded. "I'll grab my bike."

"Take that sampler with you when you go."

I spun around in the doorway. "Dad, no! It belonged to *Mama's* family. We can't pawn... We just can't. Besides, Miss Arlene said you should think about it for a couple days."

"I don't *need* a couple days, and I sure as gravy don't need needlework."

My shoulders dropped. "What if Kooky Klinch was right about the sampler being a treasure map? If we found it—"

"She wasn't." Dad tugged on a T-shirt stained with oil blotches—souvenirs from his last fight with Evrol—and moved past me into the hall. "And don't call her Kooky. She was just a delusional ninety-eight-year-old lady." He ran his fingers through his hair in an attempt to comb it. "Talking about treasure and feeding her cats all in the same note—and on a receipt! Take the sampler with you when you go. Be careful with the frame but hurry. They'll be closing soon. Make sure the McGinters pay you cash. I don't have time to run to the bank. I'll be working on Evrol."

"But, Dad—"

"Now." He pushed open the front door and walked out, ending the conversation.

I stood with my mouth open. How could he just quash the idea? What if the sampler *really was* a treasure map? Dad never took chances. To him, life was a grind instead of an adventure. Mama totally would've been game for a treasure hunt. For a brief moment I wondered what life would've been like if Dad had been the one to die instead of Mama. Then shame flooded over me. How could I even think that?

Pressing my lips together, I trudged to the kitchen table and picked up the sampler. The frame was bigger than I remembered— maybe fourteen inches by sixteen—but just as creepy with its grinning cherubs in the four corners. Dad and Miss Arlene were probably right thinking it was worth something. It was smooth and heavy and wanted to slide out of my hands.

I studied the bottom of the sampler to see if there was a name. Elizabeth Radcliffe sown and wrought this in Georgia in her twelfth year. There was something else too—but the fabric was so worn it was hard to read. A date? I brought the frame closer to my face and squinted. 1743 or maybe 1748.

At least I had a name and year I could research at the library next time I went.

I examined the needlework. All the colors were drained of their brightness. In the center was a building outlined in black thread, either a house or a church. There wasn't a steeple, but *something* was stitched on the roof. Maybe a bird or even a small cross? It was so faded I couldn't tell. A man stood on one side of the building near a rock and under a droopy-looking tree. On the other side was a smaller figure in a dress—probably Elizabeth—under a tree that stood straight and maybe had fruit hanging from its limbs.

The library article mentioned alphabets, verses, and "pictorial elements." I reckoned *pictorial elements* was a fancy way of saying buildings, people, and trees. The alphabet spanned the top, and numbers decorated the bottom. An alternating pattern of leaves and black birds bordered the entire piece.

Words had also been stitched near the house. I had to bring the sampler even closer to read the words.

Seeke ye first the Kingdome of God.
Stay close to all ye held dear. Matthew 17:39
Three layers of stone and one of timbre.
That which ye seekes is hear. Ezra 17:48

Elizabeth Radcliffe wasn't much of a speller. And why Eudora Klinch thought those Bible verses would lead her to treasure was anybody's guess. Maybe Kooky Klinch *was* nuttier than a pecan tree. But…

I began to put the frame into the box, but stopped. What did we have to lose? I glanced over to the foreclosure notice still on the table. We had *nothing* to lose because we were already losing everything. *If* Eudora Klinch was right, and *if* I could find the treasure, it would solve all our money problems.

I had to try.

CHAPTER 6

I CARRIED THE FRAME to my room and closed the curtains. Last year in history class I'd read all about the process used to preserve the Declaration of Independence. Humidity and daylight were a death sentence for anything old. Temperature regulators, lighting controls, humidity sensors were all done with computers and gadgets.

Under my bed I kept an ammo container about the size of a shoebox full of photos and random treasures I'd collected over the years, like the blue ribbon Miss Sanders had given me in third grade for memorizing all the U.S. presidents. The box was almost as rusted and dented as Evrol, but because it was as ugly as sin, it'd be the perfect place to store the sampler—for a little while at least. No one would suspect I'd put something of value inside. I reached under the bed, pulled the box out by one of the handles, and dumped the stuff from inside and blew out the dust.

Then I turned my attention to the sampler. "This thing's older than the Declaration of Independence." I shook my head. "And I'm about to put it in an ammo box."

I removed the frame's backing and, with the tips of my fingers, took out the fabric and gently rolled it. It wasn't soft like I expected. Kinda stiff, probably 'cause of its age. I set it in the box, put the lid on, and breathed a sigh of relief the thing hadn't disintegrated the moment I touched it.

I wasn't really stealing, after all, the sampler was mine. Dad wanted the money, and Miss Arlene had said she'd pay for the frame. Still…if I brought in an empty frame, Dad would find out and get upset with me. Ever since Mama died, he liked to tell me to face the facts. The real world was not all roses. He was bound to think I was living in a fantasy world if I set off on a treasure hunt. I had to find a replacement for the sampler. The only one I knew of was the Civil War replica Mama had stitched, and luckily it was close to the same size.

I hated the thought of taking what Mama had made to the Music Box because there wasn't much of her stuff left in the house. I wouldn't even be able to buy her cross-stitch back—not if Miss Arlene was going to sell it to a collector in Savannah like she'd said in Charlie's Diner. I bit the inside of my cheek. If I wanted to save our house, I had no choice but to swap them out. It was either kiss something Mama had made goodbye or kiss our home goodbye. Mama would approve. She'd have chosen the treasure hunt if she were still alive.

I grabbed her framed needlework sampler from Dad's room and put the wall calendar from my room on the empty nail to cover the spot on the wall. Then I scooted the fake tree that was near his side table over for extra protection and prayed he wouldn't notice Mama's needlework was gone.

Eudora's treasure-map sampler would be better off at Clemmie's or Thad's since they had air-conditioning, but it'd have to stay in my room until I could get it to one of them tomorrow. I covered the ammo box with the smelliest shirt I could find, figuring the stink was enough to keep Dad away from it, then pushed it back under my bed.

With the Civil War replica stuck inside the old frame, I walked into the kitchen and added the sampler to the stuff Dad had set aside. The grinning cherubs in the top corners stuck out over the edge of the box. I hoisted it and carried the whole thing outside.

Dad poked his head out from his workshop and waved.

I pedaled down our dirt drive.

I passed the sign Mayor Shore installed a few years back on County Road 1A next to the big rock that marked the edge of town. It was supposed to be a monument or something. Muggie told our class about it during a field trip ages ago. There was a plaque about the rock hanging in the museum that she made a big deal about. The plaque wasn't memorable, but Mayor Shore's sign was.

WELCOME TO GIFTON, GEORGIA.

ESTABLISHED 1745

POPULATION: SMALL ENOUGH FOR US TO MIND BOTH OUR BUSINESS AND YOURS!

Most people didn't even know Gifton existed. Our precolonial status hadn't earned us any mention in history books. Most people, it seemed, preferred visiting Savannah with its old stately homes and cobblestone streets. Gifton didn't have either. Our old buildings were made from tabby stone, and our streets were asphalt. Neither attracted loads of tourists.

Fifteen minutes was all it normally took to bike from my front door to town. But balancing a box of random stuff including a lamp and an antique frame made the trip a lot longer.

I reached the Music Box with three minutes to spare before they closed. Arliss hollered a greeting and then flipped the sign to the CLOSED side, and Miss Arlene dug through my box. I wiped my palms on my jeans as she looked over the sampler. She didn't say a word about the cross-stitch. Of course, back at the diner she'd hadn't had her glasses on, and the creepy frame had grabbed her attention more than the actual needlework. Still, it wasn't until they paid me $95 for everything that my insides stopped quivering. My plan had worked.

Arliss unlocked the door. "Come on, I'll walk you out."

The sun was still up but thinking about which colors to throw into the sky as it slid down and gave way to the moon.

"Nice evening, isn't it?" Arliss hollered at me.

"Yes, sir."

The town was shutting down. Mr. Russ was sweeping the front stoop of his insurance business. Miss Cornett locked the library's double doors and then headed for her car. The mayor and Muggie, who'd stepped out of the newspaper office, were arguing.

"But I want steak. A filet mignon," Muggie demanded. "I'm sick of ground beef."

Mayor Shore coughed. "We can't afford filet mignon."

"Then ask the town council for a raise." She yanked her purse higher up on her shoulder and wrenched open the car door. "Growing up, our family cook never served hamburgers. The mere thought—"

"Hey, Grady!" the mayor called. "Tell your daddy I'd like

to interview him. I want to ask him about how he felt about his inheritance."

Yeah. That's all Dad needed. The mayor to ask him how he felt. I waved to him. I'd pass his message on, though I was pretty sure what Dad would say.

Then I climbed onto my bike and waved to Arliss. "Good night, Mr. McGinter."

"'Night." He reached for the shop door and shouted, "If I know Arlene, she's calling her collector friend about the piece as we speak. She's got the beauty and the brains." He flexed a wrinkly, sagging, dark-brown arm and chuckled. "I'm clearly the brawn."

I nodded and pushed off.

"We'll have that sampler sold and mailed out first thing in the morning, or my name ain't Arliss McGinter!" he hollered over his shoulder to me.

Saturday morning brought Thad shaking me awake. "Grady! Get up!"

I rolled over and blinked. "Thad?" He'd climbed in through my open window again. He did it all the time.

I hated when he knocked out the screen and let mosquitoes in.

I groaned and rubbed my eyes. "What time is it?"

"A tinge after seven," answered Clemmie from outside. "But never mind that."

"Get dressed." Thad tossed me a shirt.

I threw it back at him and pulled my covers off. "I am dressed."

I'd slept fully clothed in case there was another break-in. I might need to chase after someone. I wasn't going to make a habit of being a chicken. I even started out with my shoes on, but they kept getting caught in the sheets, so I kicked them off in the middle of the night.

Thad jostled my side table and wobbled the lamp. "Sorry." He steadied it, but the nugget of turquoise plastic I'd found in the dirt a couple nights ago fell to the floor.

I picked it up and shoved it in my pocket.

"Hurry," urged Clemmie.

I rubbed my hands back and forth over my face. "Give me a chance to wake up. What's the rush?"

"There's something going on over at the Music Box." Thad disappeared through my open window. "Come on. The police are there now."

CHAPTER 7

THE SUN WAS BARELY up, and already the soupiness of Saturday morning's damp weighed heavy as we barreled toward town on our bikes. Even the buildings seemed to sag with the humidity. We raced onto Pembroke Avenue and skidded to a stop in front of the Music Box, spewing a fountain of dust and gravel behind us. Crime-scene tape wound from one awning post to around Deputy Oringderff's car and ended in a knot at the other post, blocking the store's entrance.

Ida Rose stood next to a card table outside the police boundary, wearing bunny slippers and a fuzzy bathrobe. Her hair was wrapped in pink rollers. Apparently, whatever had happened called for an emergency breakfast of sorts. She unloaded muffins from paper plates and handed them out to the growing crowd in typical Ida Rose fashion. Though, usually she wasn't dressed in her bathrobe and bunny slippers.

Usually.

Pockets of whispering adults huddled around. The Gifton Cooking Society ladies stood near Ida Rose, dabbing their eyes with tissues. Miss Bonnie Kline, the Gifton Savings and Loan manager, and the teller Mr. Sanchez, were a few feet away, speaking in low voices. Mayor Shore was with his wife, Muggie. He held a muffin in one hand and his fedora over his heart with the other.

Actually, everyone had muffins, except Ernie, who had defaulted to chicken nuggets which he must've brought from home. Thad had already inhaled the first muffin Ida Rose had given him and returned with two more.

"Hi, Ernie." I sidled up beside him near the front of the crowd. "What's going on?" I took a bite and savored the warm, buttery taste of cinnamon and apples. Ida Rose's muffins were almost as good as her pies.

"Don't know yet." He rocked back on his heels and nodded a greeting to Clemmie and Thad, then popped a chicken nugget in his mouth.

Charlie edged in close to us. He dropped his voice to just below a whisper. "I can't stay long. Got to get the diner ready for the breakfast crowd. But if it's news you're looking for, I heard that the Music Box got robbed last night."

Badger came up behind him. "Not robbed. Burgled. Robbery happens to a *person*. A *business* is burglarized."

I choked on my muffin.

Thad unhelpfully pounded my back twice. "Louis Kahn," he muttered.

"Who's that?" Charlie asked.

I nudged Thad out of the way. "An architect. He's cussing. Never mind him. Are the McGinters okay?"

"Yeah, are you sure you heard right, Charlie?" asked Clemmie.

Charlie pulled off his baseball cap, wiped the sweat from his forehead, and tugged the hat back on. "I'm sure. Badger here heard it from Letitia, who heard it from Winifred, who may or may not have heard it from Arlene herself. No one has ears faster than Winifred's."

"That's terrible," I said. "I saw the McGinters yesterday. What happened? Are they okay?" I asked again.

Charlie glanced from side to side, then crooked his finger, motioning us closer. "According to Winifred, in the middle of the night, Arliss heard a noise—"

"Arliss couldn't hear a cannon even if he lit the fuse," interrupted Badger. "It was Arlene that heard."

"Okay, fine," Charlie said. "The point is *Arliss* went downstairs to check it out. Then there was lots of crashing and yelling and an eerie wheezing sound—"

"I bet a plate of Ida Rose's muffins that was the bagpipes." Badger jabbed his thumbs into his front pockets.

Charlie shot him a scowl. "Don't interrupt."

I lifted an eyebrow. "Bagpipes?"

Charlie nodded. "Then Arlene ran downstairs—"

"As fast as someone who's eighty-five *can* run," Badger said.

"You done?" Charlie gave him an annoyed look.

Badger stared at his feet.

"As I was saying, Arlene ran downstairs," Charlie repeated. "The place was trashed. I heard it looked like Ophelia had chased a herd of squirrels through it." Charlie whipped off his hat and held it over his heart. "Arliss got himself hauled off in an ambulance."

"A scurry—that's what a group of squirrels is called," Badger said. "Not a herd. Unless of course it's a family, and then it's called a dray."

Thoughts jumbled and crashed in my head. "Why?"

Badger shrugged. "You'd have to ask a biologist or maybe a linguist. I couldn't—"

"I mean why did Mr. McGinter get hauled off in an ambulance?"

Charlie tugged his hat back on. "Tubas."

"Tubas?" Clemmie repeated. "That makes no sense, Charlie. You're worse than Thad trying to talk to girls."

Thad glared, but we all knew Clemmie was right.

"You know that big ol' shelf Arliss had in the middle of the store?" Charlie said. "The one holding those old musical instruments?"

We all nodded.

"He was found underneath." Badger sniffed and rubbed his eyes. "Wedged between a tuba and a sousaphone and clutching the bagpipes."

Badger gestured toward the Music Box. "According to Winifred, during the scuffle, one shelf fell against another and then another, and so on, until all the shelves in the room came crashing down."

Deputy Oringderff walked out of the Music Box. Everyone crowded closer to the police border and pelted her with questions faster than she could dodge them.

"What happened, Darla?"

"Is it true…about Arliss?"

"Has Arlene called with an update?"

The questions would've blown Deputy Oringderff back inside to blessed silence had it not been for Mayor Shore.

He jostled his way to the front, stepped up on the curb, and faced the crowd. "Folks! Folks, settle down now. Darla—Deputy Oringderff—I'm sure will try to answer all our questions. We all want to know what happened to poor Arliss."

He whispered to Deputy Oringderff and then stepped away.

She opened her mouth, but before she could get in a word, Mayor Shore stopped her.

"Hold on a minute, Darla." He searched the crowd. "Muggie—my hat!"

Muggie bustled through the crowd to her husband. He traded his fedora for a baseball cap with PRESS stitched on the front. He gave her a peck on the cheek and turned back to Deputy Oringderff. "Thank you, Darla. Go ahead."

Deputy Oringderff moved to the edge of the curb, holding her hat in her hand. "As you probably heard," she added *from Winifred* under her breath, "the Music Box was broken into last night during a burglary."

"Told you it was burgled and not robbed," Badger murmured to Charlie.

Charlie glared.

Deputy Oringderff continued. "Arliss was hurt pretty bad during this tragic event."

The crowd gave a collective gasp. Clemmie gave me a worried glance. I reckoned she was partly concerned for Arliss, but mostly worried about me. Some people figure any dance around the subject of a tragic event, particularly if you've already met death, can bring back unpleasant memories. Maybe she was right.

"We don't have the perpetrator in custody yet," continued Deputy Oringderff "but I'm confident we will. And when we do, we'll throw the heaviest lawbook we can find at him." She tucked a strand of hair behind her ear. "Questions?"

"You said *him*. How do you know it's a man?" someone asked.

"Yeah—you got him on camera?"

Deputy Oringderff tucked her thumbs into her utility belt. "We've reviewed the surveillance footage. Someone's in an overcoat. Sadly, it's grainy, obviously it was at night, but we also have a muddy boot print. It's from a *man's* boot, size 12. And since Arlene says she mopped the floor last night before tucking in, we're working under the assumption it's fresh and most likely the perpetrator's."

"I wear a ten!"

"I'm a nine and a half!"

"Got my mama's feet—I'm a seven!"

"I've been in elevens since I was eighteen!"

Deputy Oringderff rubbed her temples. After a pause she placed a couple fingers in her mouth and whistled.

The crowd settled into an uneasy silence while people eyeballed each other's shoes.

"What was stolen?" Mayor Shore asked.

Deputy Oringderff flipped through her notes. "Everything in the cash register and, uh, some jewelry. A few odds and ends. The storeroom was messed up a bit too. Nothing worth hurting Arliss for, that's for certain."

The McGinters' treasure trove of a storeroom was the

worst-kept secret in Gifton. Years ago Arliss had shown Winifred some antiques he'd bought at an estate sale. Arliss made Winifred promise to keep the storeroom a secret. Yeah, that would have been like the captain of the *Titanic* using duct tape to fix the hole. Soon the whole town knew—down the hall, the second door on the left was where they kept the good stuff.

Muggie faced Deputy Oringderff. "Surely this was done by an out-of-towner who figured the Music Box for an easy target. No one here would *ever*… We all love the McGinters. Maybe the town can offer a reward? For information?" She elbowed Mayor Shore in the ribs as he scribbled in his notebook. "Put it in the paper and make sure the whole county hears."

"Or just tell Winifred," Clemmie muttered.

Deputy Oringderff stepped closer to the edge of the curb and ran her hand over the edge of her hat. "We'll investigate all possibilities, and *we will* find out what happened."

"*Amen!*" Roland Spears bellowed.

A chorus of amens followed from the crowd.

Deputy Oringderff whistled for attention once more. "I need all of you to keep your eyes open and report anything suspicious so we can make sure this doesn't happen again."

The crowd began to thin. My stomach grumbled for more than a muffin, though I felt a bit guilty for caring about food when Arliss was in the hospital.

The radio on the deputy's shoulder squelched out something unintelligible.

She pushed the button on the side and asked dispatch to repeat. As the words came through, her face fell.

"Hold on, folks!" she called. "Wait a minute. Come back." She sighed. "Arliss didn't make it. This has now turned into a homicide investigation."

CHAPTER 8

"OH NO," CLEMMIE WHISPERED. She reached out and held my hand, and I let her.

Thad let loose with another architect's name.

"Didn't make what?" asked Badger.

Charlie elbowed him. "Arliss died, you idiot."

Whispers and sniffles circulated all around us.

"He was in the prime of his life." Badger sniffed and wiped his eyes.

"Wait." Thad whispered to me. "Wasn't he like eighty-seven?"

Eighty-seven or not, I had just talked to him the night before. He had been joking...and loud and full of fun. And someone had taken that away from him...and from Arlene. Memories of the day I learned of Mama's death flooded my mind. My chest tightened. I needed to leave.

"Let's go," I said.

Clemmie pointed at my feet. "Your shoe's untied. We'll meet you by the bikes."

Thankful for a chance to concentrate on something, I bent down. "Don't leave without me."

Deputy Oringderff tapped me on the shoulder as I grabbed my laces. "Grady, may I talk to you for a minute? Don't worry, you're not in trouble. I'm hoping you can help me."

"I guess." What I wanted was to get away as far as possible. But I double-knotted the lace and stood.

She took a notebook from her front pocket. "I heard you were the last person in the Music Box yesterday. Did anything out of the ordinary happen while you were there?"

"No, ma'am. The McGinters bought some stuff Dad sent in, and then Mr. Arliss walked outside with me while Miss Arlene got on the phone."

Deputy Oringderff repeatedly clicked the top of her pen. "I know this is probably hard. Did you see any strangers hanging around afterward or someone acting suspicious?"

I thought back to the previous evening. "Not really. I remember Miss Cornett locking up the library. And I spoke a little to Mayor Shore. Mr. Russ was on his front porch, and there were some other people looking at stores, but nothing…weird."

She made notes. "I understand. Thanks—this is helpful."

She looked up and smiled. "One last thing. Before Arlene left in the ambulance with Arliss, she told me that sampler you brought in yesterday is gone."

The sampler had been stolen? My mouth went as dry as sawdust in Dad's workshop.

Deputy Oringderff flipped to a new page. "Arlene was too distraught to describe the piece, and I really don't want to have to bother her now. If you can tell me what it looked like, that would help, if we're able to track it down."

Someone was after the treasure. Between the attempted break-in at our house and what happened at the Music Box, it was the only logical explanation.

~~~~~~

I described the gilded frame with the creepy cherubs, and with a pang of guilt, I told her what I remembered about the sampler— being super careful to not mention it actually had been Mama's— then hurried to join Thad and Clemmie. I quietly told them what Deputy Oringderff had said about the sampler as we got our bikes.

"No way!" Clemmie gasped. "The treasure map got stolen?"

Thad pushed up his kickstand. "What treasure map?"

"Yes—well, no." I threw a glance over both shoulders. "Not really," I whispered to Clemmie. "I swapped samplers out."

"What treasure map?" Thad repeated.

"You swapped it? With what?" asked Clemmie.

"One Mama had made." I climbed on my bike.

Thad groaned. "Would someone please tell me *what* treasure map?"

"If you weren't always thinking about your stomach or drawing houses or going to baseball games, you'd know what he's talking about," Clemmie said.

"I'll fill you in," I said. "But not until we're farther away." I sped off with Clemmie and Thad racing to catch up.

A few onlookers still lingered in front of the Music Box, but even as we raced down Pembroke Avenue, I could see most of the town had piled into Charlie's Diner. No doubt gabbing about Arliss, Arlene, and the break-in.

Once we hit the isolation of the county road, I skidded to a stop and waited for them to circle back around. I told Thad all about Mr. Burns's visit and the sampler we'd inherited. "And there's something else. I wanted to tell you yesterday but you both were out of town, and then with all the chaos this morning, I clean forgot." I leaned in, which was silly because there was no one else nearby, but I felt safer for doing it. "Someone tried to break into our house Thursday night."

Thad's jaw dropped. "What?"

"Nuh-ah!" Clemmie said.

I quickly told them about the creeping shadow and the crowbar Dad found, and then showed them the turquoise plastic I'd discovered by our door that I'd shoved in my pocket that morning.

"What do you think it's from?" Thad asked, pinching it between his thumb and finger.

I shrugged. "Don't know. It could be part of anything it's so small. It's the size of my fingernail."

Clemmie snorted. "That's because it is a fingernail. Duh. The press-on kind."

"Eww." Thad dropped it back in my hand.

"That's a pretty popular color, so good luck matching it to a specific person. Besides, it could've been there for ages, just buried in the dirt and got kicked up with people running around" She kicked her bike pedal back and forth. "Do you think whoever tried to break into your house was after the sampler?"

"I didn't know what to think at first. But now? Eudora Klinch dies and leaves Dad and me an *alleged* treasure map. Though it's not really a map—more like a riddle. But that doesn't really matter. Then, that *same* night, someone tries to break into our house. The next day, Dad tells me to sell the sampler at the Music Box, and then they get robbed." I stared at them. "That's an awfully long string of coincidences."

Clemmie grimaced. "But Deputy Oringderff said a *man* broke into the Music Box. The fingernail you found—if it's even related to your attempted break in—belongs to a woman. It can't be the same person."

"Unless they're working as a team," Thad said. "Like Bonnie and Clyde or Romeo and Juliet."

Clemmie gawked at him. "Your mouth should sue your brain for nonsupport."

We started pedaling again, but slower so we could talk.

Thad rode between Clemmie and me, arms crossed, not touching the handlebars. "I reckon it was an out-of-towner like Muggie said. People drive in all the time to look at silly antiques. Twenty bucks says Deputy Oringderff catches whoever it was."

"Unless of course they're long gone. They could be in Florida or South Carolina by now."

"I don't think it was a stranger." A sickening feeling filled my stomach. "If you're a robber, you break into a store, force open the cash register, grab money, *maybe* take some jewelry to hock later on, and *scram*. You wouldn't waste time wandering around the place, right? You wouldn't know to sneak into a back room and then run off with embroidery—heavy frame and all. It makes no sense."

"Now that you mention it, that does seem kinda weird." Clemmie glanced at me. "I've watched enough cop shows to know robbers want to get in and out fast."

"But if the thief was really after the sampler like you say, why take the money and jewelry too?" asked Thad.

"Maybe to hide the fact the sampler was what he wanted?" Clemmie said. "By taking a bunch of random stuff he could mislead the police. Misdirection, the cop shows call it. Throw them off his scent. Whatever."

I nodded. "So, the thief has to be someone who not only knew Eudora said the sampler was a treasure map and left it to us, but who *also* knew we sold it to the McGinters, and that they kept mail-out orders in the storeroom."

Thad scowled. "But that means the thief is from…"

"Gifton," finished Clemmie.

"Whoever stole the sampler thinks they have a real thing," I said. "And they were willing to murder Arliss for it."

CHAPTER 9

WE PULLED UP TO my house and I dropped my bike into the yard. Thad threw his bike down next to mine. "So let's see this thing." Evrol was in the drive.

"Dad's home. I can't show it to you here."

"Go get it and then meet at my house," Clemmie said. "I bet Mama will make us some pancakes or something. Dad's teaching a weekend class, so it'll just be us." Dr. Powell taught psychiatry at Georgia Eastern University, and Mrs. Powell was a dietician who always reminded us that breakfast was the most important meal of the day.

Clemmie grabbed the ammo box from my hands a split second after she opened the front door. She threw a glance over her shoulder. "You go chitchat with my mama and Thad. I'll hide this in my room."

I followed the smell of turkey bacon to the kitchen at the back of the house. Clemmie was right. Mrs. Powell had a huge breakfast spread ready and pumped us for information about what had happened as we fixed our plates. She had only just heard—from Winifred, of course—since she'd been on a conference call earlier. We told her everything about Arliss, but nothing about the sampler.

Even though I was starving, I found it hard to eat, and I wasn't the only one. All three of us picked at our food. The news of Arliss's death had squelched any of our normal joking, and uncharacteristic silence hung in the air. I took a sip of water and avoided the gaze I knew Clemmie was giving me. We helped wash up and then quickly disappeared into Clemmie's room to examine the sampler.

She opened the door to her big walk-in closet and yanked the pull chain. Light illuminated the mess. She delved into the back, her voice fading in and out as she talked. "I read up on samplers when I left your place the other day. It was actually very inter—" She was swallowed up by her shirts and jeans as she rummaged deeper. She emerged holding the ammo box she'd hidden for me and was still talking. "Is not outside the realm of possibility."

"Say again?" Thad plopped into her beanbag chair.

She sighed. "Do you ever listen?"

He rolled his eyes.

I shrugged. It was pointless to say she'd just told her closet more than she'd told us. I walked to the window and closed her curtains, dimming the room. "Sunlight's not good for old stuff."

"What I *said* was the history of samplers is actually pretty interesting, *and* it's not outside the realm of possibility that there could be a hidden message in the one Eudora left you," Clemmie said. "One of the articles I read online—from a museum, not some doofus site—mentioned *some* samplers contained symbols that meant stuff. Kind of like coded messages."

"Coded messages? About what?" Thad asked.

She put the ammo box on the carpet and sat crisscross next to it. "Political junk, religious beliefs, relationships. Stuff like that."

"Did the article mention if samplers were ever treasure maps?" I knelt next to her as she opened the latch. I hoped Clemmie would answer yes, because if so, that would've ended a lot of my doubts.

She snorted. "Nope."

Thad pushed out of the beanbag chair and joined us on the carpet. "What kind of symbols?"

"Everyday stuff people wouldn't blink at." Clemmie's face twisted like she was trying to remember. "Could be the kind of bird or tree or flower you'd stitch. A weeping willow might mean mourning, grief, or sadness. Different colors meant different things. And if a sampler had a lot of acorns stitched on it, it might mean the family was loaded."

I took out the sampler and carefully unrolled it on the carpet. Not an acorn in sight.

My heart dropped a little.

"Okay, but couldn't it also mean whoever sewed it liked weeping willows or acorns?" Thad asked. "They didn't all have hidden messages, right?"

"Sure." Clemmie grinned. "But that takes all of the fun out of it, don't you think? I mean if I had to sit and sew something for hours and hours, I'd totally sneak in a message."

We bent over the old fabric.

I pointed to the tree that the small girl stood under. "Is that a weeping willow?"

Thad shook his head. "No. But this one is." He tapped the tree near the man. "See how the branches droop? That other one might be a fruit tree of some kind. I think those are red dots." He frowned. "Maybe it's an apple tree?"

"Or cherry," Clemmie said.

"There's so much here." I sat back and blew out a puff of air. "We got a house or maybe a church or school, I can't tell. Thad, you're the architecture guy. What do you think it is?"

He leaned in. "It's so faded it's hard to be sure."

I groaned. "There's a rock, people, a weeping willow, a fruit tree, all these birds, and leaves. And then the alphabet and the numbers. What if it all stands for something else?"

"Don't forget the Bible verses," Thad said.

We turned our attention back to the sampler.

Seeke ye first the Kingdome of God.
Stay close to all ye held dear. Matthew 17:39
Three layers of stone and one of timbre.
That which ye seekes is hear. Ezra 17:48

Thad huffed. "People sure loved the letter e back then. What they'd do? Just stick it at the end of any word they wanted?" He pointed. "She does it with 'seeke,' 'kingdome,' and what is that word—'timbre'? Does she mean wood, like timber?"

I shrugged. "Probably. The British spell 'centre' and 'metre' with the r and the e switched. Other words too."

"And look how she spelled 'hear' and 'sown,'" Clemmie said. "Those are the wrong words—homophones...unless maybe that's how they spelled them a couple hundred years ago?"

"Maybe, or maybe she was a bad speller, but that doesn't actually solve anything," I said. "Where's your Bible, Clemmie?"

She jabbed her thumb behind her. "Bedside table."

I grabbed it and brought it back with me while she and Thad talked.

"So, here's our plan," Clemmie said.

"Typical," muttered Thad. "Who put you in charge?"

"Nobody—but hush up and listen."

I tuned them out and ran my hand over the leather cover while they argued. Up until a couple years ago all I had was a kid's Bible. Then, when Mama died, I'd taken hers. Dad wasn't reading it. Most of the margins were filled with her notes from Sunday sermons, and reading them made me feel close to her—the dog-eared pages in particular. I figured she read those the most.

I flipped to Ezra and searched for chapter 17.

"The only way we'll figure out what the hidden message is and what's just regular old decoration is research," Clemmie said. "We need to make a list of everything on the sampler."

I scowled at the Bible. There was no chapter 17. Ezra only went to chapter 10. I double-checked the sampler, but I'd read it right. I turned to Matthew.

Thad snorted. "Has anyone ever told you you're bossy?"

She frowned down at his sneakers. "Tie your shoe. You're gonna trip on that loose lace." She skipped right back to making a plan. "Then, we'll split up the list and research to see if the things have a meaning or if they're simply a bird or a tree or something."

"I wouldn't be a real friend if I didn't tell you—about being bossy, I mean," Thad said.

She snatched a pillow and threw it at him.

"Y'all." I closed the Bible and sat back on my heels. "I think I found our first clues."

CHAPTER 10

THAD DROPPED THE PILLOW he had aimed at Clemmie's head. "What?"

"The verses," I said. "That old-timey writing isn't exactly easy to understand, so I wanted to compare the verses to a modern version." I kicked off my hand-me-down shoes and moved into a more comfortable position. "Elizabeth stitched 'Matthew 17:39,' but Matthew 17 only goes to verse 27."

"Were there more verses back in the old days?" Thad asked.

"You need remedial Sunday school." Clemmie leaned back. "So, she made a mistake—maybe she had dyscalculia and put a nine instead of a six. Did you try verse 36?"

"*Somebody* wasn't listening." Thad nudged Clemmie. "Grady just said Matthew 17 only goes to verse 27." He smirked. "If you want to be a good boss, you have to open your ears."

Clemmie smacked him on the head.

"Besides," I said. "She does it *twice*. Ezra 17:48 doesn't exist either. I doubt it's a coincidence. Whatever these are, they're not Bible verses."

Clemmie bit the side of her lip. She does that when she's thinking hard. Last year in math I saw her teeth a lot during the geometry unit. "Then what do those numbers mean?"

"I don't know." I scooted back against her footboard. "Think of all the things we use numbers for." I ticked ideas off on my fingers. "Addresses, bank accounts, money—"

"Phone numbers?" Thad said.

"Not back in the 1700s, goof," Clemmie said.

"I'm kidding... Lighten up."

"What if it's...a code?" suggested Clemmie. "Wait here."

She hurried to her desk and yanked a sheet of paper and pencil from the top drawer. Thad raised his eyebrows and shrugged at me as she bent over and scribbled.

Clemmie returned and wiggled in between Thad and me, carefully scooting the sampler closer to me. She dropped the paper on the floor in front of us. Numbers one through twenty-six were written in a column, with a letter of the alphabet next to each number. "What if it's a code where a letter of the alphabet is assigned to a number? Read me the numbers, Grady."

I rattled them off.

"Slow down!" she said, scowling up from her paper. "I need time to look them up."

I paused on first verse, Matthew 17:39. "Seventeen."

She ran her finger down the paper. "That's a *Q*." She bit her lip. "Oh, that can't be a good start. Not many words begin with *Q*."

Thad pointed to her list. "The alphabet only has 26 letters, which means there's nothing for 39."

Clemmie's shoulders dropped.

"Maybe we should break up the numbers," I suggested. "Try one, seven, three, and nine for the first verse, and one, seven, four, and eight for the second verse."

Clemmie consulted her paper and wrote. "*A, G, C, I, A, G, D, H*." She moaned. "That makes even less sense than a plain old *Q*."

We focused on the letters. I tried rearranging them in my head to see if they formed any words, but all I came up with was *ACID GAG*, with an *H* left over.

"Maybe the numbers are map coordinates or...actually they probably hadn't mapped the place out back then..." Thad's voice faded.

I groaned. "There are too many options."

"We'll figure it out." Thad gave us his glass-half-full grin. "Besides"—he nudged Clemmie—"Miss Bossy here has a plan."

That was Thad—confident and optimistic. I wanted to be

full of hope like him, but ever since Mama's accident, like everything else in my life, hope was something I couldn't afford a lot of. The hope I did have, I had to guard well.

I rested my head against Clemmie's footboard while she repeated her plan about making a list of the images on the sampler and researching their possible meanings.

"We need to find out as much as we can about Elizabeth Radcliffe," I added when she finished. "Eudora Klinch too." I glanced at the clock on Clemmie's bedside table. "I've got to head home soon."

Thad and Clemmie used their phones to take photos of the sampler and promised to give me a copy. I got another sheet of paper from Clemmie's desk and jotted down every image I found. When I finished, I carefully returned the fabric to the ammo box.

Before handing it back to Clemmie, I looked at them both. "Y'all have to swear you won't tell anyone about any of this. Whoever broke into the Music Box thinks they have the right sampler. If they find out it's a fake, and we have the *real* one, there could be *real* trouble."

Thad glanced at Clemmie and then to me. "Do you think the treasure is legit?"

"*Someone* does," I said, "and they're willing to kill to get their hands on it."

CHAPTER 11

THE NEXT DAY WAS Sunday. Dad dropped me off at the front steps of church and sped away—something he'd done since Mama died. He wasn't exactly on speaking terms with God and hadn't walked through the doors of the First Community Church of Gifton for the past two years. The place could've been called the *Only* Community Church of Gifton, or even the *Only Church of Any Kind* in Gifton, but I reckon whoever named the house of the Lord probably didn't think that proper even if it was accurate.

It being Sunday, and the library being closed, I couldn't research the sampler images, but I *could* ask Pastor Jeremy about the fake Bible verses.

Pastor Jeremy was younger than our last guy—by a long shot. I'm pretty sure our last minister had witnessed the parting of the Red Sea. Pastor Jeremy was only in his thirties and bald as a cue ball, but what he lacked in hair, he made up for in biblical know-how. I was pretty sure there wasn't a thing about the Good Book he didn't understand.

I tried to listen to his sermon, but my mind traveled a hundred different directions, and my attention kept sliding from the pulpit to the watch next to me on Roland Spears's wrist. The minute hand seemed to fight against gravity as it gruelingly worked its way up from the bottom. I'd catch a random sentence here and there like "'You shall know the truth, and the truth shall set you free,'" but I had no clear idea about what Pastor Jeremy preached on.

He finally stepped away from the pulpit and signaled to Mrs. Crutchley, who hobbled to the piano and all but drove the keys through to the floor with her enthusiastic pounding of "Praise God from Whom All Blessings Flow."

As she struck the final chord, Pastor Jeremy climbed to the stage and stood by his pulpit once more. "Before we end, I'd like to announce that Arliss McGinter's funeral service will be held on Tuesday at four o'clock. He was a much-loved member of this town and church and a pillar of our community."

Murmurs and nods rippled through the pews. Miss Arlene sat near the front, flanked by Ida Rose and Winifred, and though her back was to me, I could tell she was dabbing at her eyes by the way she lifted her handkerchief.

Pastor Jeremy continued. "I hope y'all will come and support Arlene through this difficult time."

More nods.

Roland turned to me. "Probably not how Arliss ever imagined he'd meet his maker."

Probably not how any of us imagined we'd meet our maker, but I kept that thought to myself.

Pastor Jeremy ran a hand over his bald head. "Of course, a reception will be in the fellowship hall afterward, courtesy of Ida Rose and the Gifton Cooking Society."

"Amen!" Roland boomed.

The pastor exited out the side as usual to head for the front of the church. He always stood there with the doors open, letting the sunshine in and the congregation out, shaking hands and visiting after his sermon.

When I finally reached him, Winifred was already pumping him for information. The small green hat perched on her maroon curls made it look like Pastor Jeremy was talking to an unripe eggplant. I caught the words "Arlene," "misfortune," and "tragic," and for good measure she threw in something about "financial woes."

"Now, Winifred." Pastor Jeremy patted her hand. "Gossip only leads to—"

"Gossip? I would never! I'm merely sharing a *concern*," she said. "It's medicine for the soul."

Pastor Jeremy shook his head. "Er...I think you mean it's *laughter* that's good medicine. And do you know what else makes people feel better? Flowers. I'd like your opinion on the flower beds." He was a master at changing the subject. He led her down the front steps of the church to the sidewalk and pointed toward a number of rosebushes. "Don't those fragrant blooms look lovely?" He leaned in. "Mrs. Verreault was hoping to plant marigolds next to them. She loves marigolds. What do you think?"

Winifred stepped back and gaped at him. "Marigolds? Gracious, no—that won't do. Not at all. They are without a doubt the most misbehaving annual. Quite dreadful." She grabbed his arm. "Something else should be planted instead." She breathed in and out purposefully. "I know—lavender. *Definitely* lavender." She released his arm. "Don't worry, Pastor. I'll find Mrs. Verreault and tell her myself." She flew off in search of the marigold-loving-but-soon-to-be-disappointed church secretary.

He turned to me and winked. "Mrs. Verreault really *was* planning on marigolds. I hope she forgives me."

I grinned. "Can I ask you a question? It's kind of a Bible question, but not really."

"Well, that's an intriguing statement."

We walked back up the steps, against the flow of people leaving.

We stopped at the top and he leaned against the railing. "What do you want to know?"

Even though I'd thought about the riddle and the sampler during most of the sermon, I wasn't sure how to ask without giving away the fact I had the real sampler. Not that I suspected the good pastor of breaking into the Music Box. But still, I didn't want *anyone* to know. It was too risky.

"Uh...well, it's sort of a poem I came across. It gives Bible references, but they don't really fit." I'd repeated it so many times yesterday I had the words memorized. "The first part is supposedly from Matthew 17:39. 'Seek ye first the Kingdome of God. Stay close to all ye held dear.' Then after that is Ezra 17:48. 'Three layers of stone and one of timbre. That which ye seeks is here.'"

He rubbed the back of his neck. "That's definitely weird. You're right. Those references don't exist, and that Matthew verse isn't even the real thing. 'Seek first the kingdom of God and his righteousness; and all these things will be added unto you,' is the actual verse. It's from Matthew 6:33. And I don't know about that other—the one about stone and...timber, you said? It sounds familiar but I can't pinpoint it." He looked toward the parking lot and gestured with his head. "Your dad's here."

I turned. Evrol's engine sputtered and coughed out black smoke from the closest parking space. Pastor Jeremy gave Dad a big wave. Dad returned a quick, unhappy nod.

Pastor Jeremy pushed off from the railing. "Give me a couple days and let me see what I can find out, okay?"

I nodded. "Thanks."

~~~~~

On the drive home, Dad and I rode in silence. I prayed he wouldn't ask me what Pastor Jeremy and I talked about. While I didn't think he paid any real attention to the sampler, I didn't want to take the chance, and I didn't want to lie. Mama had been a stickler about that. Always tell the truth, she'd said. It was one way I could honor her memory. It'd be easy, as long as Dad didn't suspect anything.

We rolled down our dirt drive. Dust floated up behind Evrol's tires and hung in the air. Dad parked and took the keys out of the ignition, then leaned back in his seat.

"We need to talk, Grady."

My stomach clenched. He knew. He'd found out I'd switched samplers. I was toast. No, scratch that. Worse than toast. I was grits—the instant kind without cheese.

I fidgeted with the hem of my shirt. "About what?" I asked quietly.

He let out a deep breath. "The foreclosure."

My shoulders dropped with relief, which was dumb considering that Dad *actually* wanted to discuss how we were losing our home.

"Oh, that." I shifted to face him. "We've got time, haven't we? I've heard those things take months. It's not like you get something in the mail and then you're out next week."

"That wasn't the first notice." He cleared his throat. "The foreclosure process *has* been going on for a while. I didn't tell you because I didn't want to cause worry. A kid your age should be playing video games with your friends, hanging in the woods, riding your bike—stuff like that. But you've seen it, so I'm not going to pretend you didn't. You probably have questions." He started to bite his nail but saw the rim of black oil from working on Evrol and lowered his hand. "Do you? Have questions I mean."

"Are we really being kicked out?"

"Yes."

"How long do we have?"

"A couple weeks."

"Is there any way to stop it?"

"Not unless we win the lotto."

"But you said you were just selling land and that would catch us up on the overdue—"

"I know. I tried. But it's a small town. No one's looking to move out here. No one wants our land." He picked imaginary lint off his jeans. "We're going to lose the house."

"Where will we go?"

"Well, we won't live in Evrol...not yet. There's a KOA campground in Anaston."

"Anaston! That's so far." My heart was beating in my neck. "I have to leave Thad and Clemmie?"

He stared straight ahead. "I've talked to Clymer Hines and he's going to lend us his camper. Too hot for a tent in the summer. But the camper has AC. We'll be fine. And Anaston's a bigger city. I'll be able to find steady work." He glanced over at me. "We'll be in an apartment by winter."

Emily Dickinson could take her stupid hopeful canary and go fly off a cliff.

CHAPTER 12

TWO WEEKS.

Two I-better-find-the-treasure-or-life-as-I-know-it-will-end weeks was all the time I had to save our house and stay in Gifton.

No way was I going to tell Thad and Clemmie about the foreclosure...not yet. I'd read a book last year where this kid told his best friend he was moving, and his friend stopped talking to him because he was so upset. I didn't want that to happen with Thad and Clemmie and me. Not that it would. But I couldn't be sure, seeing as none of us had ever moved before. I'd just have to find the treasure. Then I'd never have to find out how Thad and Clemmie would react to my moving.

The library opened at nine o'clock, so at eight forty-five Monday morning I jammed a notebook into my backpack, along with the list of images from the sampler, and raced on my bike toward the center of town. Even though I'd be on my own, I itched to start researching like I had a bad rash. Clemmie had gone with her dad up to the university, and Thad's family was celebrating his grandma's birthday at her nursing home in Valdosta. He'd warned me yesterday he'd be gone for the whole day. Nothing and nobody moved fast at Sunshine Valley's Home for the Elderly. At least he'd get cake.

As I rounded the corner of Pembroke Avenue, Mayor Shore hoisted the flag up the pole in front of the courthouse library. I rode onto the grass, slowed to a stop, and leaned my bike against the trunk of one of the big oak trees that lined the street.

He saluted the flag before he turned to me. "Morning, Grady."

"Morning, sir." I waved and then dashed up the stone steps.

Miss Cornett, the librarian, sat at her desk and peered up from her coffee cup. "Grady! My first patron of the day." She smiled. "And my favorite. What are you looking for, sugar?"

Miss Cornett always called me *sugar*...or *honey bee*. And when the seasons changed, I knew to expect *pumpkin* and *angel*. The silly names didn't bother me because Miss Cornett was super nice and she called everyone those names, except the adults. That'd be weird.

"Not a book this time, ma'am. Just research—looking up some history stuff."

She lifted her mug and sipped. "You must've inherited some of Eudora's genes."

"Ma'am?"

She set down her mug. "She was a historian. Didn't you know?"

"No, ma'am." I thumbed behind me. "I'll be on the computers."

"Take your pick."

I hurried toward the back wall. All the computers, except one, faced large windows and had views of the courthouse lawn. They'd been set up that way so there wouldn't be a glare on the screens. But it also meant anyone could come up from behind and spy on you. I wanted privacy, so I chose the one computer that faced the inside.

I took the list from my backpack, flattened it on the desk, and then opened my notebook. For the next two hours I read and made notes. I typed every image from the sampler into the search bar and recorded possible meanings. The library filled up with people, but I didn't care. My screen was safe from prying eyes.

Cherry tree?—Prosperity, health, happiness
Apple tree?—Prosperity, love
Weeping willow—Mourning, loss, sorrow, bereavement

House/church/school—Maybe nothing. Lots of samplers
had buildings
Alphabet across the top—Pretty normal for samplers
and most had them
Blackbirds/Crows/Ravens—Temptation, death, bad
luck, infection, evil, war (look into this more!!)
Boulder/Large Rock—Nothing, it's a rock (duh)
Oak leaves—Bravery
Numbers 1-10 across the bottom—Like the ABCs,
most samplers had them

When I finished, I tucked the list safely in my backpack and then focused on Elizabeth Radcliffe.

I typed her name in the search bar. Two names appeared right away. One was a college professor in Utah and the other owned an art gallery in New York. I tried *Elizabeth Radcliff* without the *e*—after all, the British were always tagging *e*'s at the end of words when it didn't seem necessary, but that didn't help either. Thad had mentioned an ancestry-tracking website a couple days ago, so I tried that. Over 14,000 Radcliffes popped up. I scowled.

Miss Cornett walked over with an armful of books. "Finding what you need, honey bee?"

"Not really." I slumped back into the chair.

"Something I can help with?"

I didn't want to let her know the real reason I was searching. She'd been in the diner when we got the sampler. She might remember Elizabeth's name.

I decided to tell her just enough to be honest but not enough to be risky. "I'm working on our family tree and researching some long-lost relatives—the Radcliffes." I looked innocently at her.

If she recognized the name, it didn't show on her face. Instead, she smiled sympathetically. "And you're not finding anything?"

I shook my head.

"Were the Radcliffes from here?"

"I don't know for sure, but I think they were."

She thought for a minute, then gave me a conspiratorial grin. "Let me shelve these books, and then meet me at the reference desk. I have a few tricks up my sleeve that might work."

Ten minutes later, Miss Cornett rolled a chair up to the reference desk. "Let's see what we can do." She set her coffee mug down. "Give me the last name again."

"Radcliffe—with an *e* at the end." I feigned trying to remember, like it wasn't right at the top of my head. "I *think* her first name was Elizabeth. Maybe. I think."

She typed the name into her computer. "Churches back in colonial times—and even churches now—kept records of births, deaths, marriages, and such. Our archives go back to just a few months after the town was founded. Many places don't have records from that long ago. They're often lost to fires, floods, or gnawing rodents. But we're lucky." She paused, scanned the screen, and then clicked a link. "The Gifton Historic Society scanned in all the old records about ten years ago. They even photographed every grave marker in the cemetery. They wanted to document as much as they could since many of the older graves were becoming harder and harder to read from weathering and age."

Grave markers. Cool. I held my breath in anticipation.

She frowned at her screen. "Hmmm. Nothing. Not in the births register anyway. But that doesn't mean Elizabeth didn't live here. It only means she wasn't *born* here. Let's try deaths. Hold on." Her fingers clicked and clacked so quickly I couldn't figure out what she was typing. She scoured the screen for a couple moments. "I don't see *anything* on an Elizabeth Radcliffe." Miss Cornett peered at me. "Perhaps she wasn't from Gifton after all. Can you remember any other names?"

I pictured the sampler in my mind. There *weren't* any other names. Only the stitched figures of Elizabeth standing under a tree on one side and a man standing near a large rock on the other. Probably her dad. But no other names. Unless you count the names of the men who'd written the Bible verses.

And with that thought, an idea formed.

Maybe her dad...

I wondered...

I hoped...

"Could you try Matthew or Ezra Radcliffe?"

She arched her brow.

"I think I remember hearing someone mention those names...at some point..." I shrugged. "I–I might've misheard though," I stuttered.

"It's worth a shot." Her fingers flew across the keyboard. "Eureka!"

CHAPTER 13

I DARTED TO MISS Cornett's side of the desk, but then jerked to a stop. "Am I allowed back here?"

She waved my question off and scooted her chair over so I could see the screen.

We were looking at a scanned image—an old page with handwritten names and dates filling columns. The paper looked like the kind Mama and I had tea-stained in third grade and then burned the edges to make it look like old parchment. But the faded ink meant that this must be legitimately old—not tea-stained. All the writing was super fancy too, and difficult to read.

Miss Cornett pointed to one name. Matthew Ezra Radcliffe. But the thing that made my skin prickle with goose bumps was found in the column next to the name. *Year of Death,* 1748. The same numbers Elizabeth had sewn into the sampler next to the fake verse, Ezra 17:48!

I swallowed. "What is this?"

"It's a page from the church's deaths record." She toggled to the next screen. "The whole register was scanned."

Row after row of handwritten names and dates scrolled past. There were lots of names. Too many for me to count.

She pointed. "Look! There's a Charlotte Radcliffe listed— died 1746. Maybe she was related to Matthew Ezra."

"Maybe," I said.

"Or to...who did you ask for first? Elizabeth?"

The sampler was dated 1748. If Charlotte was Elizabeth's mama, that would explain why Elizabeth and her dad were the only two people she'd stitched. I quickly did the math in my head. If Elizabeth was twelve when she sewed the sampler, she and I had been about the same age when our mamas had died. We had more in common than I expected.

"Are there pictures of their graves?"

"Hold on." She leaned forward and typed. With a satisfactory tap of the last key, she leaned back, interlaced her fingers, and turned to me. "Voilà." A black-and-white picture of a small, plain grave marker appeared. It was almost the same size as the pillow on my bed. Probably as comfortable as it too. The stone leaned at a slight angle.

MATTHEW EZRA RADCLIFFE

SOLDIER, HUSBAND, FATHER

B. 1710

D. 1748

"And see here," Miss Cornett pointed. "Charlotte Radcliffe's grave is next to his. So, yes she was his wife."

CHARLOTTE FELICITY RADCLIFFE

WIFE, MOTHER

B. 1710

D. 1746

She leaned closer. "We know they had children—or at least a child—because it says *father* and *mother* on their gravestones. So, maybe Elizabeth was their daughter? If that's the case, she was most likely born *before* they moved to Gifton—because she's not listed in the church's births register."

I thought about the dates on the gravestones. "He died just two years after his wife."

"And so young," Miss Cornett said. "Only thirty-six and thirty-eight."

Yeah, well, Mama was young when she died too. I still had

my dad. When Elizabeth's dad died, she had no one. What would I do if I became an orphan like Elizabeth had?

Maybe Miss Cornett saw what I was thinking, because she said, "Of course, disease, war, and your basic day-to-day living took out a bunch of folks. Life was really tough back then."

"And their graves are in the Gifton cemetery?"

"Yep." Miss Cornett faced her screen. "Plots A-35 and A-36."

I grabbed a pen from the desk and wrote the numbers on my hand. "Thanks!" I laid the pen down and scurried to get my backpack from the floor.

"Wait. Where are you going?" she asked.

"To check them out." I swung my backpack onto my shoulders.

"Not today, I'm afraid. Arliss's service is tomorrow, remember? You know how Mr. Thornton gets when there's a funeral."

Lester Thornton was the cemetery caretaker. When he prepped for a burial, he refused to let people in and padlocked the gates. He *claimed* it was to keep everyone safe since there were digging equipment, folding chairs, and a big canopy, not to mention a deep hole, but I think he liked feeling important every so often. Couldn't really blame him. And since it was the *only* time the gates were ever locked—he didn't even lock them at night—people didn't mind.

My shoulders fell, and the backpack slid to the floor with a thud.

"Don't worry," Miss Cornett said. "The Radcliffes aren't going anywhere."

That was true.

"Does your computer say anything else? Like how they died or if there was any other family?"

She scrolled down. "I don't see anything. Colonial-era graves didn't usually have much information on them."

Neither did current ones. Mama's marker was like the Radcliffes'. It had her name, when she was born, when she died, and her favorite Bible verse, Ephesians 2:8.

Miss Cornett printed off the images of the death register and the grave markers and handed them over.

I took the papers. "Thanks, Miss Cornett. This is really helpful."

She stood. "I wish more kids took an interest in their family history. There's so much we can learn from our ancestors."

There was so much I wished I'd learned from Mama before she died. I thumbed behind me to the row of computers. "There's a few other things I still want to check. Thanks again for everything."

She waved me off and I hurried back to the computer in the corner. Now that I knew what the 17:48 number meant, I wanted to figure out how the 17:39 reference fit. It was a puzzle, that was for sure.

Mama had loved puzzles. She bought a new puzzle magazine every month when the Piggly Wiggly got the new magazines in. She would've been all over this sampler riddle. Thinking of her reminded me of something she told me once about a thing called Occam's razor. Razor meant rule—who knows why—and this old philosopher had a rule that basically said the simplest explanation is usually the right one.

If I used his philosophy that the simplest explanation was probably the right one, then the simplest explanation was 17:39 was also a date.

Ignoring the words *Matthew* and *Ezra*, I pounded 1739–1748 into the search bar.

An image of a calculator with =–9 appeared. Pretty sure *that* was useless information. But the articles below the calculator were full of news. The War of Jenkins's Ear was fought between 1739 and 1748. I spent a while reading, then printed more articles to take home.

I'd hit the jackpot.

CHAPTER 14

I WAS DYING TO tell Thad and Clemmie everything I'd discovered yesterday, but Dad had needed my help repairing our fence near the county road. It didn't matter the fence had been broken for weeks; it just had to be done today. It was as if he was saying, "You can repossess my house, but you can't repossess my dignity. I'll keep this property looking neat as a pin despite you saying I don't own it." So I worked all the way up to the time I had to leave for Arliss McGinter's funeral.

For the millionth time, I inwardly cussed at the fact we didn't have a telephone. I'd missed out on giving and getting loads of information, all because we couldn't pay a phone bill. I didn't mind biking over to Thad's and Clemmie's houses to tell them things because, thanks to all the biking and running, I had the best calf muscles in all of Gifton, at least according to Clemmie. But on days when Dad wouldn't let me go, it would've been nice to have a phone.

At the funeral, Miss Arlene was all tears and tissues for the first hour but settled into sniffs and dabs by the time we moved outside and the first shovelful of dirt thudded onto Arliss's coffin after Pastor Jeremy prayed. I felt terrible for her. A few weeks earlier, she and Arliss had celebrated their sixty-third wedding anniversary by inviting the whole town to an ice cream sundae party at the Music Box.

Ida Rose linked her arm through Miss Arlene's and led her from the graveside, speaking softly. Clemmie, Thad, and I followed the crowd out of the cemetery and up the steps to the fellowship hall for the reception.

The fellowship hall usually smelled like wet paper towels and hand soap, but today the aroma of cookies, cakes, and macaroni and cheese filled the air. Ida Rose's desserts were disappearing faster than Ophelia could chase a squirrel. Several round tables with folding chairs had been set up in the center of the large hall, and since Clemmie, Thad, and I were some of the last people to walk in, most of the seats were already filled.

I nudged Clemmie and Thad. "I'm going to explode if I don't tell y'all what I learned at the library yesterday, but I don't want anyone overhearing us. Let's get some food and eat outside."

"Good idea," Clemmie said.

Thad paled. "Eat outside? Like…in the cemetery?"

Clemmie and I sighed at the same time. Thad's fear of cemeteries was almost as powerful as his love of eating and architecture. The only reason he even came to funerals was for the food.

"You'll have cake and fried chicken," I reminded him.

Clemmie grinned and nudged him toward the food. "Yeah. And I'll protect you from any ghosts."

Thad took a shaky breath and stood in line with Clemmie and me.

Someone clearly underestimated the number of people expected, because by the time we got to the front of the line, the tower of Styrofoam plates had dwindled away. The stack had been replenished with whatever could be found in the church cupboards. Bright-green and yellow paper plates with the scrawled words CONGRATS ON YOUR RECENT PROMOTION! were all that remained.

Clemmie picked one up. "It's oddly appropriate in a way."

"Hurry before all the good stuff vanishes." Thad breathed in sharply. "Muggie brought out her buttermilk pound cake from the back."

Clemmie eyed his loaded plate. "You and your stomach."

I picked up a red plastic cup filled to the brim with sweet tea, and Clemmie and I left, balancing our plates and drinks. Other people had come outside and sat scattered under shade trees. We picked a solitary spot under an oak, and within minutes, Thad caught up with us.

"It's weird to think last week was Kooky Klinch's funeral and now here we are again," Thad whispered as he sat on the grass and balanced his plate on his lap. "If you think about it, the deaths are kind of related. If Eudora hadn't died and left you the sampler, Arliss wouldn't have died." He crammed a cookie into his mouth.

"Classy," Clemmie said. "Blame a dead woman who can't defend herself."

"Nah. It's not her fault," Thad mumbled through his food.

More like it was my fault. If I hadn't sold the sampler to the Music Box, Arliss would still be alive. The heaviness of that guilt turned the food in my mouth to mush. I drank my tea to wash it down.

I pulled my note-filled papers from my back pocket and smoothed them out next to my plate. "Clemmie, get your phone and find the photo of the sampler, will you? I want to have something we can look at." I checked to my left and then to my right to make sure no one was listening, and then leaned in. "I know what those numbers from the fake verses mean."

Thad jerked, almost knocking over his tea. "You solved it? What are they?"

"Sheesh, Thad." Clemmie grabbed the cup before it spilled onto her plate and soaked her cookies. "Chill. He's going to tell us."

The news seemed to help Thad forget his cemetery issues. At least for a little bit.

I nodded. "When I typed the numbers in the search bar, like I was entering a date—no colons or anything—just 1739 dash 1748," I paused for dramatic effect, "the War of Jenkins's Ear popped up."

Thad scowled. "That weird war Mrs. Maragos crammed in the last couple weeks of school? What's the big deal?"

I flicked an ant off my plate before it got any closer to my brownie. "Mrs. Maragos *said* there'd been skirmishes and raids in our area during that time. People steal stuff on raids, right? I mean, that's kind of the point. I bet during one of the raids, Elizabeth's dad took something valuable and buried it. Its location is hidden somewhere in the sampler's riddle. If we solve the riddle, we find the treasure." I sat back, satisfied with my delivery of the news.

"Whoa, whoa, whoa." Clemmie put her hands up. "How do you know the numbers are even dates? They could be anything. Maybe it's a coincidence they matched the dates from the War of Jenkins's Ear."

Thad huffed. "Whose side are you on, Clemmie?"

"There aren't sides, doofus. But at the speed Grady's jumping to conclusions, he'll break his neck."

I figured Clemmie would be a hard sell. She liked having all her squirrels lined up on a tree branch before coming to a decision. Which, if you've ever tried to line up squirrels, you'd know is near impossible.

While they ate, I told them I figured out that *Matthew* and *Ezra* were the first and middle names of Elizabeth's dad.

Clemmie side-eyed me. "So you're saying the books of the Bible refer to her dad, and the Bible numbers point to the dates of the war?"

"Exactly. And like I said, the War of Jenkins's Ear was *all* that popped up on the internet when I typed in those numbers. Nothing else. Just article after article about the British and the Spanish fighting each other. So, the treasure has to have something to do with her dad and the war." I rubbed my neck and grinned. "See? No broken neck after all."

"I'm still trying to remember what Mrs. Maragos said about the War of Jenkins's Ear," Clemmie said. "I only half listened."

"Look it up on your phone."

A few seconds later she pulled up an article. "Fought between Britain and Spain, *yada, yada, yada*... Didn't really have a whole lot to do with Captain Robert Jenkins's ear being cut off." She looked at us and grinned. "But I'm sure that didn't *help* matters." She continued reading. "A bunch of stuff having to do with trading, taxes, *blah, blah, blah*, and lots of skirmishes on land and sea."

"See. Skirmishes! That's what I'm talking about," I said. "I bet you anything Spanish gold was taken during one of those."

"Hmm." Clemmie's brow furrowed. "I guess it's *possible*."

I could tell she thought some squirrels were still running wild. "There's more," I said. "Certain images on the sampler also refer to the war."

She brushed crumbs from her fingers. "Like what?"

I scooped a forkful of mac and cheese and pointed to her phone. "Go back to the image of the sampler. See the border of birds and leaves? The leaves mean bravery, and you have to be brave to fight in a war."

"Please tell me you have more to go on than that," Clemmie said.

I held up a finger. "I'm not done. I'm pretty sure those birds are crows—they're black, and well..." I shrugged. "They look like crows."

Clemmie enlarged the image. "Agreed."

Thad peered over her shoulder and gave me a thumbs-up.

"According to what I read, most birds have nice meanings. Goopy stuff like love, eternal life, and hope." I scrunched my nose. "But crows symbolize *bad* things."

"What kind of bad things?" Thad asked before chasing down a ginormous bite of brownie with a huge chunk of meat loaf.

"Death and *war*. Here's the weird thing though. No one in

their right mind would've used crows purely for decoration. It'd be like a taking a picture today and photoshopping in a bunch of vultures, and then mailing it out as the family Christmas card."

"Eww." Clemmie grimaced.

Thad grunted. "That'd be weird...unless you're part of the Addams family or into zombies or something. Why do you think she did that?"

"That's what I'm trying to tell you! The sampler points to war. The War of Jenkins's Ear."

Clemmie waved off my response. "Okay. What else?"

"You know, along with being bossy, you're also impatient," Thad said.

Truer words were never spoken. I'd learned long ago that telling Clemmie to be patient was like telling a bull to ignore the color red.

Clemmie gave Thad a light punch on the arm. "Okay, so she put in her father's name, and she put in the dates of the war. And she put in the crows. But it could just be that her dad died in the war or something. There's nothing yet that means money or treasure. No acorns. So why do you think there's a treasure?"

I swallowed my food and pointed to her phone. "There are two trees in the sampler. Her dad is standing under a weeping willow. That stands for mourning. He died, right? She'd definitely be mourning. *But*, the tree that Elizabeth is standing under, which

I'm 99.9 percent sure is a cherry tree because of the tiny red dots, means wealth and"—I checked my notes—"prosperity and new beginnings." I looked at her. "Wealth? Prosperity? Elizabeth is hinting at treasure. She has to be."

"Maybe," Clemmie said, clearly not convinced.

I pulled a sheet from my stack of notes and laid it on top. It was a diagram with clues from the sampler, each with an arrow pointing to the center, where I'd drawn a bunch of dollar signs. I tapped each clue on my paper while I spoke. "We have dates—*tap*—that match the time of the war. Crows—*tap*—that symbolize death and war. Leaves—*tap*—that mean bravery. And the cherry tree—*tap*—that represents wealth. We have to look at the whole picture because that's what Elizabeth left us—a picture. When you look at the whole thing, it points to the war and treasure."

Clemmie chewed on her lower lip and plucked at the grass. I held my breath. Finally, she met my gaze. "Okay. It makes sense." She grinned. "I agree. No broken neck."

"And it's not like we have a bunch of other theories anyway," Thad said while sneaking a cookie off Clemmie's plate. "What did you find out about Elizabeth?"

"Zilch," I said. "Miss Cornett checked to see if the library had anything and came up with squat." I grinned and leaned closer to them. "But get this, both of Elizabeth's parents are buried here in the cemetery."

"Like *this* cemetery?" Clemmie asked.

"Yep—I want to look for them as soon as we're done eating."

Thad burped.

"Gross. Excuse you," Clemmie said.

Thad grinned. "I'm done."

"And I've lost my appetite," she said.

"Then let's walk around the cemetery. We need to find the Radcliffes' graves." I lowered my voice. "Because I think I know where the treasure is buried."

CHAPTER 15

I STOOD AND BRUSHED food crumbs from my shirt and pants.

"You what?" Clemmie's dark eyes grew round as she gripped my wrist and dragged me back down. "Tell us!"

I shook my arm loose and straightened. "Not until we find the gravesite because I have to make sure of a couple things first."

The faint outline of A-35 and A-36 was still on my hand, though I didn't need it; I remembered the Radcliffes' plot numbers. I didn't know how the graves were organized, and while Lester Thornton would, I didn't want to ask. No one needed to know we were searching for graves or treasure. I wanted to have the treasure in my hands before anyone knew we were looking for it. And…I was about to make that happen.

The older graves were closer to the church. That much I knew.

There were a few exceptions—like Arliss's—but that's because the McGinter family had bought a chunk of the cemetery before Arliss was even born, and that old family plot was still not full. I only knew that because I'd overheard Miss Arlene talking about it to Pastor Jeremy. Arliss's final resting place was so close to the church entrance Miss Arlene could practically sit with him in the front pew each Sunday morning.

Mama was buried farther away, but at least she was on the same side as her favorite stained-glass window, the one with Jesus ascending into the clouds...or maybe he was descending back down to gather up his people. No matter which direction he was headed, the colors were beautiful, and she'd loved them.

"Won't we look suspicious wandering around?" asked Thad, nodding toward the other mourners eating outside.

I shook my head. "Nah. Let's walk slow and keep talking. People will think we're just strolling through and chatting."

Clemmie grinned. "I got a better idea. Stay here." She ran back inside the church and returned minutes later with a large piece of paper and a stick of pink sidewalk chalk. "Now if anyone asks, we'll just tell them we're making rubbings. Nothing suspicious about that."

"Perfect," I said. "Let's go."

We started close to the front and took our time, stopping

at each gravesite to read the engraved name. Many stones were so weathered it was impossible to know what they said. Large gray spots of lichen and patches of moss clung to many of the older stones. One of the graves had a carved face on it. Might've been an angel or maybe even a skull, but at this point I couldn't tell. And with each impossible-to-read gravestone, the worrying realization that Matthew's marker might be just as deteriorated and unreadable as the ones I'd already seen nagged at me. It had looked fine in the library photo, a little tilted, but that was years ago. Who knew what it looked like now?

When we got to the end of one row, we went to the next and headed back the other way. Markers were different shapes and sizes. Some were flat and low, while others were narrow and tall and leaned at odd angles. I had to squat to see who was buried there, while others were taller than me.

On the fifth row, Thad elbowed me. "Just tell us already. Where is the treasure? I got the willies walking over all these people's graves."

"I found it!" Clemmie said, crouching next to a gravestone. She traced Matthew Radcliffe's name with her finger. "The words are pretty worn, but it's not too bad, considering how old it is."

"Don't touch it!" Thad said.

She grinned over her shoulder at him. "Why? You afraid

I'm going to break it?" She stood and wiggled her fingers. "Or summon up a ghost or something? Oooohhhh!"

Thad shoved his hands into his pockets. "No...maybe. Just leave it alone. Walking around a graveyard is bad enough. Touching the gravestones ..." He whistled. "That's a totally different kind of mojo."

I knelt next to her. Finally. Here it was. The stone tilted a smidge to the right, just like in the photograph. A blotch of lichen covered most of the R in Radcliffe, but it was definitely his final resting place. Spanish moss draped over the top like a handful of spaghetti noodles. I picked up the stringy mess and tossed it behind me.

"Well, we found the grave." Clemmie faced me. "You said you know where the treasure was. Spill it."

I glanced to my left. The stone wall that bordered the cemetery was just a few feet away. Perfect—so far, so good. I stood and motioned Clemmie and Thad closer to me. Part of me was afraid if I shared my idea, Clemmie would find a flaw with my logic and the whole thing would go up in flames faster than Atlanta during the Civil War.

"Remember how Elizabeth sewed a building in the sampler, and there was that verse that said 'Seek ye first the Kingdom of God'?"

"Yes," they both said.

"I'm pretty sure the building is the church. That verse is also talking about the church. You know—Kingdom of God and all. And the 'three layers of stone and one of timbre' could be talking about this stone wall." I pointed. "See how it's built up in layers?"

Clemmie opened her mouth, but I kept talking. "Let me finish. The 'timbre' part—remember the British spell things weird—could mean timber, like wood." I pointed up. "Look at the trees we're standing under now. It's the canopy layer. "

"Yeah, but how can you be sure about this spot?" asked Clemmie.

"Because of the second line of the riddle. 'Stay close to all ye held dear.' Her folks are buried right there. She hid it *close* to her parents, who she probably *held dear*. And don't forget the dad is standing under a weeping willow—means mourning, remember—and he's near a stone. That could be a hint to look at the stone wall near where he's buried."

Clemmie raised her brow.

"Plus, 'close' has two meanings." I pulled my notes from my back pocket. "'A continuous containing wall, completely surrounding the churchyard, of which the greater area is the parish cemetery.'"

Clemmie scrunched her nose in disgust. "If you think I'm going to help dig up a grave—"

"No, no—I don't think it's *in* Matthew Radcliffe's grave." I walked to the low stone wall and patted it. "I think it's *near* it. Maybe in this section somewhere." I spread my arms out wide and paced off several steps. "Here's why: if you needed to hide something, you'd want to put it someplace permanent. Like, you wouldn't hide it under a tree, because that *could* get chopped down and you'd never find your stuff again. But a stone wall isn't going anywhere, and even though it's short, you could crouch behind and bury something without being seen."

"Why did she hide it in the first place?" Thad asked.

Clemmie read the inscription on the grave next to Matthew Radcliffe's. "That's her mama's headstone, isn't it?"

I nodded.

"So, her mama died before her daddy and then she became an orphan the day he died." She turned to Thad. "She probably didn't know what to do. Think about it. Orphaned. Scared. She had nobody left and was probably worried about what would happen to her. Where was she going to live? *How* was she going to live?" Clemmie stared at the two headstones. "If that treasure was the only thing she had, and maybe even the last thing her daddy had given her, she'd want to keep it safe. At least until she knew what was going to happen to her. I can understand why she buried it."

I thought back to when Mama died. What was the last thing she'd given me? Probably some laundry to put away.

No.

I thought harder.

A hug. Cheesy, right?

She'd given me a hug that morning…and then she never came home. If I could take that feeling of her warm arms wrapped around me and hide it somewhere safe, where no one could ever take it away, I would do that, like Elizabeth Radcliffe had done with her father's treasure.

I waited for their reaction. "Well?"

Clemmie bit her lower lip. "Not to burst your bubble or anything, but if she hid it when her daddy died, she probably came back and got it later. It might be gone."

I had hoped she wouldn't bring that up. Since the day we got the sampler, I'd wondered the same thing, but I *needed* to believe the treasure still existed. I sighed. "Eudora was still looking for it, so she must've thought it was still here."

"Yeah, well, she also believed *the flowers* were the treasure," Clemmie muttered.

"Miss Cornett told me Kooky was a historian. Maybe she came across something in her research that made her believe Elizabeth never came back for it."

Thad grunted in agreement. "Out of curiosity, why do you say it was Elizabeth who buried the treasure? What makes you think it wasn't her daddy who buried it, told her where, and then croaked?"

I sat on the wall. "It doesn't matter who buried the treasure, but I'm pretty sure it was Elizabeth because of the words she stitched. The more I reread the riddle, the more I realize she loved to play with words. Look at the sampler."

Clemmie sat next to me and pulled up the image on her phone. I pointed. "See the bottom."

"Elizabeth Radcliffe sown and wrought this in her 12th year," Clemmie read. "What of it?"

"Not *sewn*, like she stitched something, but *sown*, like she'd *buried* something. Exactly like you would sow a seed. What if she's saying—in a sneaky way—that she buried the treasure and then made the sampler?"

Clemmie peered at the image and then whistled. "Gotta hand it to you, Grady, I wouldn't have caught that. I would've chalked it up to another British spelling or Old English or something."

Thad rubbed the back of his neck. "But why sew the sampler in the first place? If Elizabeth's the one who buried the treasure, then she knows where it is."

"For the same reason pirates made treasure maps." Clemmie said. "She probably didn't want to forget where it was. How was she supposed to know when she was coming back? Could be years."

"That's a good point," I said. "Or maybe the sampler was a way to both remember the treasure *and* honor her dad." I shrugged. "Girls were kind of expected to sew those things back then. My guess is she decided to insert a hidden message in symbols."

Clemmie faced me. "What do we do next?"

That wouldn't be easy. "We can't dig during the day. Someone will see us." I looked around and confirmed no one was near us. "It's not like Pastor Jeremy—and *definitely* not Lester Thornton—will let us dig here, even if it's only against the wall and not an actual grave."

"Uh...so if not in the daytime, you mean...we'll dig at night?" Thad squeaked a little when he said it.

"*Tonight*, to be exact. At midnight., when no one else will be around"

Clemmie gasped. "We can't do that! It's totally illegal."

"It's only illegal if the gates are locked and there's a No Trespassing sign somewhere," I argued. "But Lester never locks the gates when there's no upcoming funeral, and I don't see a sign, do you?"

Clemmie bit her lip and scanned the churchyard. "Well, no."

Thad grimaced. "I can't. I have to...uh...wash the...hamster," he sputtered.

Clemmie put her hands on her hips and stared at him.

I pushed off the wall. "Listen, I wouldn't ask if it weren't important." I figured if they knew we were about to lose our home, they'd rush to the cemetery—dirty hamster and all—but I couldn't bring myself to tell them about the foreclosure notice. I didn't want them to think Dad wasn't a good man. "It's not only about finding the treasure, I promise. It's more than that. Trust me, please."

Clemmie relaxed and turned to me. "I'm in." Then she stared at Thad again.

Thad examined his fingernails.

"I said, I'm in. How about *you*?" She poked his chest.

"Me?" He rubbed his chest and gulped. Thad's fear of ghosts was nothing compared to his fear of Clemmie. "I'm…in?"

"Yes," she said. "Yes, you are. And I'll bring you some sunflower seeds."

"Oh," Thad said. He gave me a weak smile. "Good."

CHAPTER 16

"WHAT ARE Y'ALL UP to?" Miss Arlene's voice pierced through the cemetery's quiet.

The three of us spun around as Miss Arlene hobbled toward us from one row over. We'd been so focused on our conversation that we'd stopped paying attention to who or what was around us. Had she heard? Did she know? Would she tell Pastor Jeremy our plan?

"We're making rubbings!" Thad blurted, pointing to the blank paper in Clemmie's hand.

Clemmie nodded and knelt next to the stone opposite Matthew's. "Yep, and uh, we found a great one." She leaned in. "LITTLE EDDIE, 1803" she read. "Oh, and there's an inscription. HE SMILED AND SAID, 'MAMA, I'M GOING.'" She scowled and sat back. "Well, that's depressing. Maybe we'll go with a different one."

"You three are *just* the young folks I was looking for." Miss Arlene made it over to us and clasped my wrist with her thin hand, probably to keep from falling over on the uneven ground. She breathed in deep. "I want to thank y'all. It's a big job and I truly appreciate it."

I had no idea what she was talking about, but it didn't sound like she'd overheard us. She patted my hand, then turned to Clemmie. "Your folks graciously offered your services. Such a sweet lady, your mama…insisted you children would be happy to help." She blinked vaguely. "Bless you, dears."

Clemmie clearly had inherited her bossiness from her mama. She shot a curious glance at us and shrugged. "I'm sorry, ma'am," she said. "Help with what?"

"Cleaning up the Music Box. Things are everywhere and nowhere. Such a mess." Miss Arlene squeezed my hand tighter. "I suppose you heard about all the shelves falling like dominoes?"

We all nodded.

"So much is broken. I'm not the spring chicken I used to be and can't lift most of what's currently scattered all over the floor." Her lower lip trembled. "Now, Arliss—*sniff*—he—*sniff*—he could've lifted anything. He was so strong and robust."

I resisted the urge to tell her that Arliss could've probably lifted our *spirits* if he were still with us, but that would be about it. He was about as strong as a lace doily.

"But of course, now—" She broke down into sobs and releasing her grip on me, cried into her hankie.

Thad focused on the ground. Then the sky. Then his hands. Clemmie rolled her eyes at him and helped me guide Miss Arlene to the closest tall gravestone to lean against.

Miss Arlene wiped her nose before tucking her hankie into her sleeve at her wrist. "I'm okay now. Anyway, as I was saying, I need you kids to help me clean up now that the police have released the crime scene." At the mention of the crime scene, she broke down crying again. Out came the hankie once more.

We waited.

After a bit she blew her nose. "I'm sorry. I really wanted to be strong, but today isn't going as planned."

"I know how you feel," I said quietly.

And I did. According to what some well-meaning folks said to me on the day we buried Mama, the funeral meant I could now "move on." Like after simply burying someone, life would somehow magically be fine. But what they didn't get was that when her coffin was lowered into the ground, a good chunk of me went with it. You can't move on when you're not all there.

Miss Arlene's eyes met my own. "I know you do." She cleared her throat. "Tomorrow morning? Say eight o'clock? And I'll pay you, of course."

We'd be digging all night at the cemetery. The idea of then

spending the whole day cleaning and hauling stuff around the Music Box made me want to steal some shut-eye right then and there. But the hope of finding the treasure boosted my energy. If it was where I suspected, we'd be rich. I could hire a whole cleaning crew to help Miss Arlene and then I'd spend the day sleeping…maybe in a new bed…in an air-conditioned house.

"Sure," I said.

Plus, maybe we could find out who killed Arliss. I figured Deputy Oringderff and her team had scoured the place good, looking for clues, but if the Music Box was as messy as Miss Arlene claimed, there was a chance they'd missed something. Something maybe we'd find while cleaning.

Miss Arlene tucked her hankie back into her sleeve. "Would y'all mind walking me back inside? It's farther out here than I thought, and this lawn is too lumpy for someone my age." She prodded a nearby clump of grass with her cane. "I wobble like a dizzy chicken over these tufts. Thaddeus, dear, take my arm."

Thad paled. We all knew crying ladies made him nervous, and Miss Arlene was as stable with her emotions right now as she was walking on uneven grass. Luckily, he was saved by the timely arrival of Winifred Paulin.

"Arlene, dear, thank goodness I found you." She paused and smiled at the four of us. "Taking comfort here at my ancestor's grave." Winifred never let an opportunity to talk about her ancestors pass her by. Come to think of it, she never let an opportunity to *talk* pass her by.

I glanced at the tombstone. Miss Arlene's dress covered up the last name, but I could make out REVEREND JOSEPH. The famous reverend she loved to talk about.

Then batting aside the moment of silence, Winifred looped her arm through Miss Arlene's. "Now, Arlene," she whispered with all the softness of an army tank, "you'll *never* guess what I heard from Badger about Lester's sister." Her voice grew faint as she guided Miss Arlene back toward the church. "I figured you'd want to know—as a matter of concern, of course—since she was…"

"That was close," Thad said.

"Meet me back here tonight at midnight," I whispered. "Bring a flashlight and shovel."

CHAPTER 17

THE SOUND OF DAD snoring at night was almost as loud as him using the table saw during the day. Despite my confidence he was fast asleep, I grabbed a flashlight and snuck out my bedroom window instead of the front door. No reason to invite trouble. I took a shovel from the toolshed and jumped on my bike. Balancing the shovel across my handlebars, I raced into the night toward town. Even though clouds were rolling in, the moon sat high enough above the trees to light the road.

After tonight my life was going to change. Dad would freak if he discovered what I was sneaking off to do, but if I came home with my pockets filled with jewels or silver coins or gold doubloons or whatever, I'd be forgiven. A gust of wind blew across me as I turned into the empty parking lot and pedaled toward the cemetery.

The moonlight struggled to make its through the thick tree canopy that blanketed the church building and cemetery. The lights on either side of the double doors were on...sort of. One was burned out and the other flickered, but it was enough to see Thad pacing near one of the large oak trees just inside the stone wall. His bike lay on the ground with a shovel next to it.

"Is Clemmie here yet?" I whispered.

"Coming in hot," she said, skidding to a stop next to me.

"Any trouble getting away?" I passed through the gate and laid my bike next to Thad's.

"A little bit," Clemmie said. "Mom and Dad were watching some dumb documentary so I couldn't sneak through the living room to the garage."

"How'd you get your bike and shovel?" asked Thad.

"Climbed out my window and shimmied down the tree. Just got a couple splinters." She gripped the handlebar with one hand and grasped a shovel with the other. "Y'all ready to find treasure?"

The breeze picked up, scattering leaves and bringing the smell of rain.

Thad frowned at the clouds. "Maybe we should do this another time. Feels like it might storm."

Clemmie raised her brow at him.

"We just need to hurry," I said.

Thad grimaced and picked up his shovel. "Well, the sooner

we're done, the better. Ernie Dixon swears he saw the ghost of the old library director wandering around here a couple years ago."

"Why would Mr. Barnsworth haunt the cemetery and not the library?" I walked toward the Radcliffe graves, leaving the flickering orange glow of the church behind me.

"Maybe he was headed for the library," Thad said, casting a wide-eyed glance over his shoulders as he turned on his flashlight. "Ernie says he was carrying a stack of books and muttering about the nonfiction section being out of order."

Clemmie snorted. "Sounds like Barnsworth. Miss Cornett's much nicer. But don't listen to Ernie. I wouldn't trust someone whose idea of a great meal is a plate of microwaved chicken nuggets. That 'ghost' was probably indigestion. There's no such thing as spirits or apparitions or whatever you want to call them."

"Says you," Thad muttered. "And who says 'apparitions' anyway?"

The trees moaned with the wind. We stopped cold.

I was never one to believe in ghosts like Thad, but standing in the middle of a cemetery at midnight made my stomach swirl like a washing machine. Tree limbs stretched like bony fingers against the night sky. By now, more clouds had gathered, and the moonlight had grown fainter. But there was enough for shadows to stretch from gravestones. Shadows long enough for someone to hide in.

"Come on," I said. "I don't want to get caught." I lined up where I wanted to start digging along the wall nearest to Matthew Radcliffe's grave. "Let's stick as close to the wall as we can. I think that's what Elizabeth would've done—you know, to avoid being seen."

Clemmie nodded. "We should take turns. One of us can hold the flashlight and keep a lookout while the other two dig. And every few minutes we can switch." She stopped and scowled at Thad. "Tie your shoe before you trip and land on a grave."

"Miss Bossy strikes again." He obediently knelt and grabbed his laces.

He was right, but Clemmie's idea was a good one.

"Thad, you want to dig or hold the flashlight and keep guard?" asked Clemmie.

No answer.

"Thad?" She nudged him with her foot. "Dude. Pay attention."

"Check out this grave. Samuel Ransom, 1784 to 1797. He was only thirteen when he died. Our age." His flashlight cast eerie shadows on his gloomy face. "Kids aren't supposed to die," he added quietly.

I almost told him mamas aren't supposed to die either, but I didn't. I just picked up his shovel and handed it to him. "Come on, man. Let's dig. If we're lucky, we'll be walking out of here with treasure in no time."

For a while, the only sound was the wind and the *shhhnk* our shovels made as we drove them into the ground. The smell of fresh dirt filled my nostrils. I used to love that smell. Mama did too. She was the happiest when she was gardening. Now the smell only reminded me of the day we buried her.

"This is hard work." Thad wiped his sweaty forehead with his shirtsleeve. "You're going to share, right?" he blurted. "I mean, yeah, you pretty much solved everything on the sampler, but we're helping with the dirty work."

Clemmie elbowed him. "Let him buy a cell phone first. Sheesh."

"Of course I'll share." I had no doubt there'd be plenty to go around. People didn't make treasure maps for dinky amounts of loot. It had to be something huge.

Thad grinned. "Think there'll be enough for season passes to the Braves? That's what I'd buy."

"If we're lucky, you can rent a party suite for the next decade to watch a bunch of guys hit a ball with a stick," Clemmie said. "I'm thinking bigger, like a private jet or something."

How those two ever managed to be best friends was beyond me.

"Get what you want." I dumped another shovelful of dirt on our growing pile. "I only need enough to save our house and—"

"Wait." Clemmie pointed the flashlight beam on my face. "When you say, 'save our house,' you mean—?"

"Move your light, Clem!" I shielded my eyes. *Crud.* I hadn't meant to mention the foreclosure.

"Sorry." She pointed the beam back toward the hole but kept looking at me. "What's going on?"

Reluctantly I told them about the bank notice.

"That's why we *have* to find the treasure. And soon. It's the only way Dad and I can stay."

"You can't move away." Thad held my gaze. "The three of us... It wouldn't be... I mean we've always..." His words fell to the ground. "You can't move. That's all. You just can't."

"How much time do you have?" Clemmie asked.

I didn't want to answer. If I told her, that would make the truth seem more real than I could stand.

"We've got time," I lied. "Let's just keep digging."

Thad pushed his shovel back and forth between his hands. "But what about—"

"What in the name of all that's holy are you three doing?" A stern voice pierced through the darkness.

My heart fell to my kneecaps and then shot to the top of my skull.

Thad let a few architects' names fly.

I spun around. Pastor Jeremy stood on the other side of

the low wall holding a flashlight, a fishing pole, and a tackle box. Ophelia, grasping a large stick in her mouth, sat next to him.

My mind went blank. "Uh..."

"Okay," he said, "I'll start. *I* was night fishing." He held up the pole and tackle box. "Didn't catch much but still had fun. Now it's your turn." His voice was calm, but, considering what we'd been doing, I wasn't sure how long his patience would hold.

I gulped. "Uh..."

"A few more details would be helpful, Grady." He set his fishing pole and tackle box on top of the stone wall "I'm waiting."

I groaned and jammed my shovel into the dirt. My cheeks burned. Frustration and embarrassment flooded over me. No way in the world would he let us continue to dig, and I couldn't believe we got caught.

"Well?" Pastor Jeremy raised his brow. His eyes darted from Clemmie to Thad to me, but came to a stop on me. Something told me he knew I was the one calling the shots.

I hadn't thought ahead to make up some other story for being at the cemetery. I remembered the one verse I'd actually heard Pastor Jeremy say on Sunday. "'You shall know the truth, and the truth shall set you free.'"

Maybe just flat out telling him the truth about the situation *was* what I should do.

My shoulders dropped. "The truth is we were looking for buried treasure."

His eyes lit in surprise. "Treasure? Here?" He scanned the graveyard. "You've decided to become grave robbers?"

"No! Nothing like that." I plopped down onto the wall. "The treasure from the sampler."

He moved his tackle box over and perched beside me. We sat shoulder to shoulder, facing opposite directions. Lightning spider-webbed across the sky, highlighting thick, dense clouds for an instant.

"Listen, Grady," Pastor Jeremy said as a low rumble of thunder replied in the distance. "I was out of town last Wednesday. I don't know anything about this sampler everyone's talking about, and if it hadn't been for an early Saturday morning phone call from Winifred telling me about Arliss, I'd still be out of town. The one thing I *do* know is that sampler sounds like trouble. Deputy Oringderff told me it was one of the things stolen from the Music Box."

A strong wind blew through the trees. A warning wind. That's what Mama called the gusts that came right before a storm hit, strong-arming their way through trees and down streets, sometimes blowing over trash bins.

I knew in my heart Pastor Jeremy wasn't the thief. I told him everything.

I told him about the War of Jenkins's Ear.

I told him about the clues in the sampler.

I told him what I *thought* the treasure was and where I thought it was.

When I finished spilling my guts, he whistled. "You really are good with puzzles. You figured out all that from a piece of embroidery?"

"Please don't be mad," I said. "We weren't going to dig up any graves—I promise. Just this area along the wall."

He put a hand on my shoulder. "I'm not mad, Grady. But… the treasure isn't here."

"What do you mean? It *has* to be here. It makes total sense."

"This church wasn't around when your sampler was sewn."

My throat tightened. "What?"

He waved his arm toward the building. "This was constructed in the late 1860s. There's a plaque on the building with the exact date somewhere. The shrubbery is hiding it. The original church was damaged during the Civil War. The bell tower and roof were completely destroyed by fire, and while the tabby stone walls weren't totaled, they needed a good amount of repair."

"I thought tabby stone was indestructible," Clemmie said.

Pastor Jeremy gave us a weak smile. "Sure, if your walls are five feet thick like St. Augustine or Fort Frederica, but the church walls weren't that generous. The folks decided after the war to rebuild the church closer to the center of town. They reused the church bell and what tabby stone they could from the original building."

Thad kicked at the ground and sighed. "Yeah, I've read that after Fort Frederica was abandoned, the tabby was cut into blocks and used for the foundation of the St. Simon's lighthouse."

Pastor Jeremy nodded. "It was a fairly common practice to reuse the stones."

Thunder crashed.

"No, you're wrong. That can't be true." He made no sense. And why was my chest so tight? I rubbed it, trying to force the tension to disappear. "Matthew Radcliffe's grave is right there." I pointed. "You must be wrong. He died in 1748. And his wife in 1746. And there are others. Thad, you found that one of the kid earlier. Clemmie—you saw it, right?"

Clemmie's beads rattled in agreement as she bobbed her head.

"Yeah." Thad hurried over to where Samuel Ransom's headstone stood and shone his flashlight on the marker. "It's right here. Graves from the 1700s. How do you explain that?"

Pastor Jeremy's soft answer held a hint of sadness. "While it doesn't happen often, cemeteries are sometimes relocated to better memorialize the dead. Especially if the current graveyard and church have suffered extensive damage—which would have been the case after the Civil War destruction." He sighed. "I'm sorry, Grady, but this stone wall, this church, and this graveyard did not exist back then. Wherever the treasure is—if it's even real—it's not here."

"They'll get kicked out of their house if we don't find the treasure," blurted Thad.

I shot him a glare that could've raised Samuel Ransom from the dead. "*That* was supposed to be a secret." Dad wouldn't want the whole town knowing about our problems. And neither did I.

Pastor Jeremy eyed me. "Grady?"

I rubbed my thumb over the rough stone wall. "Foreclosure," I muttered. Nothing else. He could figure it out on his own.

"Oh man." He rubbed the back of his neck. "The church might be able to help. Have your dad come talk to me—"

"You know Dad." I shook my head. "He won't accept help from…God."

"Help comes in lots of forms." He squeezed my shoulder.

Clemmie fiddled with a handful of her braids. "It's okay. We just need to find the location of the original church and grave-yard." She stopped. "Of course, we don't know the spot where Elizabeth's folks were buried or if there was a stone wall back then, so…" Her voice trailed off.

Pastor Jeremy swatted a mosquito. "*I* know where the original foundation is. In fact, Grady, I'm surprised you don't. It's on your property. A large slab—probably overgrown with trees and such."

"The Knee Scraper? That old foundation was the church?" My voice rose a notch.

He nodded. "That's all that's left."

Thad bit his lip. "But if the riddle means what you think it means, we need a stone wall. We've hung out at the Knee Scraper a gazillion times. There's no stone wall or anything that looks like it used to *be* a wall."

The feeling of total failure dragged my heart down to my feet. There had to be another explanation of the riddle. I looked behind me and grimaced at the mounds of dirt we'd piled up nearby. "We'll...um, put all the dirt back and, well...we'll just pray that no one notices the mess, I guess."

Pastor Jeremy stood, his forehead scrunched in thought. "You know, thanks to Winifred, I've got a wheelbarrow load of marigolds in need of replanting. This section of wall is as good a place as any for some relocated flowers." He squeezed my shoulders. "Folks need be none the wiser."

He returned a few minutes later with the marigolds. Lightning tore open the sky and rain poured down as we planted the orange flowers along the wall, covering their roots—and my dreams—and giving me one more reason to hate the smell of dirt.

CHAPTER 18

WEDNESDAY MORNING, I LEANED my bike against the outside brick wall of the Music Box just as the church bells across town chimed eight o'clock. Last night's news about the destruction of the original church still hurt, and the stupid happy ringing sound was just adding to my already sore gut.

If Dad ever learned about last night's disaster, he'd probably say being spontaneous wasn't the wisest of moves, and I could've saved myself a lot of trouble if I'd just slowed down and researched things a little bit better. He'd have been right too.

I gritted my teeth in frustration that Clemmie and Thad weren't there yet. We needed to talk about other places the treasure might be. At least, I needed to talk to them. They'd have homes no matter what conversations we did or didn't have.

Me…? Not so much.

But then Clemmie, with Thad close behind, rounded Pembroke Avenue and pedaled in my direction. I waved, then faced the large storefront window, cupped my hands on the glass, and peeked inside. Miss Arlene stood in the center of the room, cane in one hand and hankie in the other. She wore jeans and a T-shirt and had a yellow, orange, and red striped head wrap covering her hair.

Righting the toppled shelves would be the easy part. Finding the floor underneath all the fallen and broken stuff was going to be a challenge. I wasn't holding my breath about getting to the library to do research—not that afternoon at least. Maybe tomorrow if I was lucky.

"You cheated, Clemmie," Thad said walking up the sidewalk. "I said no shortcuts."

"Crossing the bank parking lot is not a shortcut," Clemmie retorted. "I just didn't want to hit the pothole on Pembroke. It's full of rainwater." She joined me at the window. "So how bad is it?" She looked inside and whistled. "Looks worse than Heather Dawn's after last year's Bingopalooza."

Heather Dawn's coffee shop doubled as the bingo parlor every Friday night. Or at least it used to until last year. Bingopalooza had always been the town's biggest game. Heather Dawn, who'd just received a delivery of nitrogen-infused coffee, decided for that evening only, all coffee would be "on the house." It was a first.

It was also a last.

The over-caffeinated bingo players abandoned their usual manners at the first victorious outcry of *bingo*. Half the crowd rushed to the bathrooms, while the other half stampeded for a refill before the next round could start. Rumor had it, someone tripped and landed on Badger, who fell against Charlie, who may or may not have accidentally yanked the fire alarm when he toppled to the floor.

Everything might've been fine if faulty wiring hadn't kicked the overhead sprinklers into high gear, shooting water from the ceiling. The drenched crowd barreled for the exit, leaving a trail of toppled chairs, overturned tables, and soggy bingo cards.

"Before we get started cleaning, we should say something nice about Arliss to Miss Arlene," Clemmie said. "It would be polite."

I shuffled my feet against the sidewalk. Miss Arlene stared blankly around the store, twisting her handkerchief. "Maybe. I don't know what to say though."

"Me neither," Thad said. "And when I do say stuff, it's usually the wrong thing."

"Just say whatever comes to mind. It's the thought that counts," Clemmie said. "She's coming!"

Miss Arlene opened the door. "Come in, dears, come in."

"I like your hair wrap, Miss Arlene," Clemmie said. "I have a similar one at home."

Miss Arlene absent-mindedly touched the scarf. "Thank you, dear. Trying to protect the hair as much as I can. You know how that is."

Clemmie nodded in agreement. "Yes, ma'am, I do."

Miss Arlene dabbed a tear from her eye and then stuffed her hankie into her pocket. "I was just wondering where to start. Such a mess." Her shoulders slumped. It wouldn't've surprised me if she yanked that hankie right back out again and bawled into it.

I cleared my throat. "Miss Arlene, ma'am?"

She tilted her head toward me. "Yes, Grady?"

"I'm really sorry for your loss. Arliss was"—my mind went empty—"uh...a fun guy," I blundered, and turned helplessly toward Clemmie.

She slowly shook her head.

Miss Arlene sniffed. "Yes, he was, wasn't he? Arliss danced to the beat of his own drum."

"Too bad *those* weren't on the shelf instead of the brass instruments, ma'am," Thad said. "They don't weigh as much, and he might've survived them."

Clemmie kicked him in the shins.

Miss Arlene patted his hand and gave him a wobbly smile. "Thank you, dear."

"We're very sorry for your loss, ma'am," Clemmie said as Miss Arlene shuffled to a spot behind the cash register. "You're both idiots," Clemmie muttered. "Just promise me you two won't start writing sympathy cards anytime soon."

Besides the shelving on the floor, old musical instruments lay strewn about. A couple spindly side tables had toppled over near the front door. One was down to just two legs, the other legs nowhere in sight. A Victorian-looking sofa—the kind that look like they belong in the lobby of a super-fancy hotel—lay on its back. The fern that sat on an antique plant stand near the cash register had taken a nosedive. Jewelry sat mixed in with power tools—none of which were antiques. Most had belonged to Dad at some point. The power tools. Not the jewelry.

I cleared my throat. "We can get this cleaned up, Miss Arlene."

She murmured. "That would be marvelous. The Music Box was Arliss's baby. He'd want me to go on running it." She bent and retrieved a small, gold handheld mirror with a crack running from side to side and set it on the counter. "Though I don't know where I'll find items to replace the damaged or stolen pieces."

I reviewed the room. "I have a general idea of where stuff goes, from bringing things in for Dad all the time."

"That's good, dear," she said distractedly.

Clemmie rubbed her hands together and got Miss Arlene's attention. "I'm sure you have papers to take care of. We'll tackle the big stuff here." She picked up a necklace and laid it next to the mirror. "If we don't know where something goes, we'll ask."

"Yes. That makes sense." Miss Arlene straightened her shoulders. "Thank you, General Clemmie. I love your plan. If one of you could bring out my little card table from the back and set up in the corner, I'll work there. That way I can answer your questions about where things go. I *knew* I hired the smartest kids in town. We'll stop around noon for lunch. The fridge is overflowing with leftovers from yesterday." She left us and went down the hall.

"General Clemmie?" Thad snorted. "You wish."

Clemmie grinned. "I like the sound of it."

"I'll get the table for Miss Arlene," I said.

When I returned, General Clemmie took control. "First, we need a path so we can walk around without breaking ankles or antiques. Then, let's move all the broken stuff to one side and the unbroken to the other, and get these shelves standing again."

We straightened, untangled, righted, picked up, and put down all sorts of stuff. If a stranger had peeked through the store window, they'd have had a hard time seeing any improvement, but we could tell it was slowly coming along. I understood why Miss Arlene thought it would take more than a day. I just hoped whatever she paid us would hold off the foreclosure a little while longer. Until I could find the treasure.

For the last couple of days, Dad had worked late into the

night and gotten up super early. That one cabinet order from the Clarke family wasn't going to save our home. We needed lots and lots of orders. I don't know who he thought he was fooling, but it wasn't me. Then again, I was hoping a couple days cleaning a store would make a difference.

Snagging a chance to talk with Thad and Clemmie about the sampler never happened. Considering Arliss had died *because* of the sampler, I'd be insensitive to mention looking for its treasure in front of Miss Arlene. Plus, if she started crying, Thad might run out in a total panic, and we needed all the help we could get. Occasionally, she'd disappear into the storeroom or office, but never long enough for the three of us to talk.

Miss Arlene tapped my shoulder a couple hours later. "Grady, dear, I need your assistance with something in the back."

"Yes, ma'am." I dumped a dustpan full of white beads, dirt, and crushed fern leaves into the trash can and followed her down the hall.

A large worktable hogged the center of the storeroom's crowded space. On my left, two ginormous wooden desks, whose sides were scarred and gouged with age, faced each other. An old computer sat on one and various papers, folders, and notebooks covered the other. Bulging shelves on the right had stuff that was probably valuable if you knew what you were looking at, but the vases and knickknacks looked like antiquey junk to me.

Everything was orderly and organized except for one thing in the center of the room.

A giant reel of packing paper had unrolled across the floor like a long, brown tongue sticking out.

Miss Arlene pointed to the floor with her broom. "I can't lift that big ol' spool any more than I can lift a marble slab. Would you put it back on the table? I want to sweep under it."

I lifted it onto the worktable.

"Thank you, dear." She pointed to an empty box next to it. "That's where your sampler was—all tucked in, wrapped as snug as a bug, and ready to go to Savannah. I was going to mail it the next day." She sighed and swept the floor. "I called the buyer this morning and broke the news to her. She was devastated of course—both for my loss and hers. I told her there's always a chance Deputy Oringderff might find the sampler." She shrugged. "Who knows?"

"Miss Arlene, can I ask you something?" I slid a stool over and rested my arms on the worktable.

She stopped sweeping. "What's on your mind?"

I stared at the table, searching for the right words. She was so calm. So…composed. After Mama's death I was furious. Chewed up and swallowed by anger.

I raised my eyes. "When Mama died…all I felt was mad. Everything in me wanted to yell. I wanted to throw things.

Sometimes I *did* throw things." I shifted on the stool. "She had this coffee mug she used every morning. It said...Number One Mom. I gave it to her for Christmas."

Miss Arlene chuckled.

"After her accident, I went into the kitchen and...umm..." My voice caught. "It was on the counter beside the sink, half-full of day-old coffee. I washed it and put in the cupboard so it'd be ready for her when she came home. Only she didn't come home. A few weeks later I opened the cupboard, and her mug was still there. But she wasn't. It was so unfair." I took a breath. "I never wanted to see it again, so I took it outside and threw it into the woods."

Miss Arlene leaned the broom against the shelves and cocked her head. "Now why do a thing like that?" Her soft voice held no accusation. Just curiosity.

"I don't know. The minute I threw it, I wished I hadn't. I found it. It had hit a tree and the handle had broken off. Now I keep it on my desk as a pencil holder." I stared at her eyes. "Anyway, you don't seem *mad*. Why aren't you *mad*?"

"Oh, Grady." She hobbled over, pulled out the stool next to me, and settled onto it. "How we react when our loved ones are stolen from us is a decision no one should have thrust upon them." She gave my hand a quick squeeze. "Especially a young one like you. The way we choose to live each day is something we must purposefully decide with each and every sunrise. Now take Arliss—always the glass-half-full type. I've always been a glass-half-empty kinda gal. A realist. A complete counterpart to him." She chuckled. "But we complemented each other like salt and pepper."

Like Mama and Dad.

"But whether you're a half-full or half-empty type of person isn't important." She leaned closer to me. "What's important is to remember the glass is *refillable*." She patted my cheek. "And that is my answer to your question. Yes, I'm devastated. Heartbroken. Hollow. Part of me is gone, and I won't get it back."

She stood and shuffled back to her broom. "But you're right. I'm not mad. I choose not to fill my glass with anger and regret, but with forgiveness, life, and hope." Her eyes watered.

There it was again. Hope. Miss Arlene obviously had the same cheerful canary Emily Dickinson had.

I wanted to fill my glass with the same thing.

I wanted to hope that Dad and I would be all right.

I wanted to hope that we could just *talk* again.

I wanted to hope that one day we'd joke around and laugh with each other.

I wanted to hope I had something in common with him.

But as much as I *wanted* to have those hopes, I didn't have them. Not yet at least.

I tucked the two stools back under the table as her words swirled in my head.

Miss Arlene finished sweeping, parked her broom, and stood in the doorway. "I'm going to heat up lunch. Why don't you get Clemmie and Thad and meet me upstairs?"

I scanned the room to see if anything else needed tidying. The fact the sampler was the only thing taken from the back room made me think my theory of the burglar really wanting the sampler was spot-on. No thief would take time to snoop around just out of curiosity.

Back in the front room, Clemmie and Thad were replacing musical instruments on a shelf. "Come on. Miss Arlene's getting lunch ready."

"I'm starving," Thad said. "All this work has made me hungry."

"You're always hungry," Clemmie reminded him.

We took the narrow hall stairway that led to the McGinters' above-store apartment. The front door opened to a living room with a well-worn sofa and recliner facing an old-fashioned TV on one side. The other side had a small dining room and kitchen. A doorway at the back probably led to the bedroom and bathroom.

Miss Arlene shut the refrigerator and set a pitcher on the counter. "Fill those glasses with ice, would you, Grady? I'll pour the tea." Tupperware containers filled with potato salad, macaroni and cheese, green beans, and thick slices of reheated meat loaf covered the counter. "After you've dished yourselves up, have a sit-down." She gestured toward the round kitchen table.

I didn't realize how hungry I was until I tasted the first delicious bite of meat loaf. Miss Arlene, Clemmie, and Thad talked about our progress while I shoveled food into my mouth. When I ate the last morsel of macaroni and cheese, I sagged back against the chair.

Miss Arlene grinned. "I hope you saved room for dessert." She thumbed behind her. "Muggie's buttermilk pound cake is by the sink."

"Yes, ma'am, thank you." I pushed my chair back.

Glancing out the kitchen window on my way to the cake, I stopped. I leaned over the sink to see better.

"What's going on, Grady?" asked Thad.

"Something's happening across the square." I waved them over. "Charlie's Diner—it's on fire!"

CHAPTER 19

WHEN WE GOT OUTSIDE, we saw it wasn't Charlie's Diner on fire. It was Badger Paulin's lawn-mower repair shop. Broken, old lawn mowers had belched out smoke for years over at Badger's, but this time the billowing color looked…different. And serious. The air stank of burnt rubber and oil.

We waited on our side of the street as Gifton's volunteer fire truck wailed past, and then Clemmie, Thad, and I dashed to the other side. The gathering crowd outside the repair shop elbowed one another asking questions and probably making up answers. Someone mentioned Ida Rose should be notified so she could bring a dessert of some kind. But at the rate smoke poured from the back of the building, I figured all we really needed were marshmallows and some skewers. The crowd parted as Deputy

Oringderff arrived. Winifred Paulin stood outside, wringing her hands as blackish-gray smoke rose from behind her brother's shop. "Where's Badger? Has anyone seen Badger?"

"I'm sure he's fine," Deputy Oringderff said. "The building doesn't look to be on fire. I think it's something out back." She hustled away and around the side.

As if on cue, Badger stumbled around the opposite corner, coughing and clinging to Mayor Shore.

"Badger!" Winifred flung herself at her brother. She hugged him and then held him at arm's length. "Where's your left eyebrow?"

Badger rubbed the bare spot on his face. "Uh..."

Mayor Shore wriggled off his fireman's coat. "Probably got singed when the fire leaped from the barrel."

The crowd surrounded Badger, hurling questions at him. Clemmie, Thad, and I stood our ground near the front. Muggie Shore elbowed past us, took the mayor's fire helmet, and handed him his baseball cap with PRESS stitched on the front, along with his small notebook. He pointed to the thinning smoke, rising from the back of the repair building. "How did this start? What happened?"

"I...uh, I was just burning some stuff in the barrel, but a spark flew out..."

The mayor frowned and scribbled notes.

"It must've landed on an oil patch and then—"

"Wait. What kind of *stuff*?" the mayor asked.

"You know. Stuff." Badger's eyes darted back and forth from the ground to the crowd. "Stuff that needs burning. Some papers, old rags, a pallet I busted up."

Deputy Oringderff appeared behind Badger wearing a fireman's gloves and holding a pair of smoldering boots. A good part of the tread on both shoes had melted into a globular mass. "Size 12?"

Winifred gasped.

Badger gulped.

The crowd gaped.

Thad nudged me. "That explains the burnt rubber smell."

"Boots!" Winifred poked him in the chest. "Badger! You nincompoop! You torched your work boots? What in heaven's name were you thinking?"

"I–I got nervous." He turned wide-eyed to Deputy Oringderff. "You said you found size 12 boot prints at the Music Box. That's my size! And everyone at the diner heard me say I wanted to get my hands on that treasure." His face paled under soot smudges. He looked as guilty as sin. "What if they thought I was the murderer!"

Deputy Oringderff groaned. "Now that you've tried to destroy evidence, of course they're—"

Badger stepped back. "I didn't try to destroy evidence. I just burned my *boots*."

"Same thing," she said, frowning.

Winifred blinked and shook her head like she was trying to clear a thought. "Badger, you mindless idiot! You *look* guilty for burning them, and now you can't *prove* you're innocent because you melted the tread off."

"Thinking's never been Badger's strength," Clemmie said under her breath.

"It's not his weakness either." Thad rubbed the back of his neck. "It's probably something he should just steer clear of."

Deputy Oringderff sealed the boots in an evidence bag. "I'm going to need to ask you some questions. Why don't we head somewhere a little less public?"

"You're taking me in?"

Whispers floated into the air and mixed with the trailing smoke.

"Did Badger...

"The Music Box?"

"Is he the thief?"

"Badger's got to be the dumbest criminal..."

"Do you think he meant to harm Arliss?"

Winifred drew herself up to her full height, which wasn't much. "Darla! You know the only thing Badger is guilty of is being stupid. Lord knows he finds new ways to show off his folly every day, but he's no criminal."

Badger hung his head.

Winifred continued. "Those might be his boots, but he didn't kill Arliss. He's not allowed to wear those dirty things inside the house, so he always leaves them on the front porch. Everybody knows that. Anyone could've taken them and worn them that night. All they'd have to do is put them back before morning."

The wall of people behind me pressed in to hear.

"He tried to burn evidence!" Deputy Oringderff guided Badger toward her car. "We need to clear up a few things, and the sooner we go, the sooner I'll get answers. If everything checks out, I'll have Badger home in time for *Wheel of Fortune*—maybe even sooner."

"*Wheel of Fortune*?" Badger straightened. "Oh, I don't watch that—I'm a *Jeopardy!* kind of guy."

Deputy Oringderff narrowed her eyes and pointed to the back seat. "Get in."

Winifred wrung her hands. "Is he under arrest?"

"Not yet." Deputy Oringderff slammed her door. "But we'll see."

~~~

On the way back to the Music Box, we debated whether we should tell Miss Arlene about Badger.

"She's going to want to know what happened. Besides, she'll

find out soon enough anyway," Clemmie said. "We might as well be the ones to break the news."

"He was Arliss's friend," I said. "What do we say?"

"She'll start crying," Thad said. "I'll stay downstairs and clean stuff."

"Chicken," Clemmie muttered. "At some point you're going to have to learn to talk to women."

"Not until I absolutely have to," Thad said.

We didn't have to tell her. Miss Arlene stood behind the jewelry counter with a phone clutched in her hand, concentrating on her conversation. We paused at the doorway.

"Oh my, Winifred…Badger?" She gasped. "Well… Yes, I… Fine. Thank you for telling me." She hung up the phone and stared at the wall.

"You okay, Miss Arlene?" I asked.

She let out a long sigh. "Not really."

In the silence I heard in my head, Winifred's words to her brother repeated over and over. *Badger, you nincompoop!* I reckoned she didn't mean it. People don't always think about what they say when they're upset. Just like Dad didn't mean some of the things he'd said to Mama's doctors…or Pastor Jeremy. That's what I told myself.

"I think," Miss Arlene said, "I'd like to call it a day. I'm tired and this news is… Well, it's a pill I'd rather not swallow right now."

"Would you still like us tomorrow, ma'am?" Clemmie asked.

She stopped and turned. "Yes, please. Same time if that works."

Before we could leave, the bell on the door jingled. "Grady?"

I spun around. "Dad, what are you doing here?"

He stepped inside. "Had a meeting at the bank. Thought I'd see if you were done."

"We are for now, but I—"

"Good. We'll put your bike in the back of Evrol."

"But I wanted—"

He swept his hand toward the door. "Let's go."

My shoulders dropped. "Dad, there's some stuff I need to do. Clemmie and Thad and I are working on something... important."

"Sorry, Grady. Not today."

"But Dad—"

"Now!"

~~~~~

I pulled Evrol's door shut and yanked my seat belt on. "Why couldn't I stay?"

"I'm glad you're helping Miss Arlene. That's good. Your mama would've been proud. I want you to continue to help—in the mornings." He cleared his throat and focused straight ahead. He pulled onto Pembroke Avenue. "We have to start packing. We need to decide what we can take, because there won't be much space in Clymer's camper. Just room for the basics."

My stomach rolled.

His lips pressed in a line. "I don't know what I'm going to do with my tools. I need most of them for work. But heaven only knows where I can store them. It's going to take a lot of time to pack them and…there's everything in the house."

"What about Mama's things? Her rocking chair—you made that. And she loved it. We can't get rid of her stuff. I won't."

Silence carried us all the way until we reached County Road 1A. "I'll think of something. I won't get rid of the rocking chair."

It was the first thing we'd agreed on in months.

He slowed on our dirt road. "You can help Miss Arlene for two more days, but after that I need you at home."

How could I find the treasure if I spent every minute helping Miss Arlene or packing at home? The mockingbird in my chest reappeared, stronger than ever. If hope was a thing with feathers, mine just molted.

CHAPTER 20

THURSDAY MORNING, I SHOVED my notes about the sampler into my backpack and prayed I could sneak in a few minutes at the courthouse library after helping Miss Arlene. I grabbed my bike and met Thad and Clemmie outside the Music Box at eight o'clock just like we'd done the day before.

Thad picked nervously at his fingernails. "I hope Miss Arlene doesn't cry today. I can't talk to women when they're acting normal, let alone when they're upset. I'll say something stupid again."

"Who said it's better to shut up and look stupid than to open your mouth and prove it?" Clemmie asked. "I can't remember."

"Oh, I know this one!" Thad said. "Moses."

Clemmie scoffed. "Really?"

"It was Abraham Lincoln," I muttered. "Or maybe Mark Twain. Not Moses."

Miss Arlene set her face in a smile and waved at us, then navigated across the floor.

"Don't say anything, Thad, and you'll be fine," I quickly added.

She opened the door from inside, keys in hand, and her purse dangling from her arm. "Change of plans. We're going on a road trip. A short one."

Clemmie and I exchanged worried glances.

Thad paled at the news. "Ronald Morris," he muttered.

While Miss Arlene *had* a driver's license, it would've been better for the whole town if she didn't use it. She owned three pairs of glasses, but she never wore the right ones for driving. The last time she climbed into her small 1965 convertible after wearing a pair, she'd taken out four potted plants and sideswiped a stop sign, before halfway parking on the sidewalk in front of Jireh's Beauty Salon.

I swallowed. "Where to?"

"Eudora's house."

I perked up. It might be worth risking my life if Kooky Klinch's house was the destination. Maybe she'd left some clues about the sampler lying around!

Thad gulped. "Do we have to?"

Miss Arlene chuckled. "Teta Lynne Greene from the Tipton County Cat Society called me last night. There's a whole load of furniture and stuff at Eudora's they want to get rid of, and they're giving me first dibs." She grinned. "For free! They just want it out of the house. I need y'all's strong arms to carry everything to the truck."

The truck.

If Evrol had a distant cousin, it'd be the old moving van the McGinters had recycled as the Music Box's delivery vehicle. Years ago, Arliss had named the thing King Kong. Of course, Badger had corrected Arliss, saying King Kong wasn't a monkey but probably a *Gigantopithecus*. How Badger could know random stuff like that and still be stupid enough to burn his own boots was anybody's guess.

Considering King Kong was built like a tank, and we had a short drive to Eudora's house, our chances of survival were fair to good.

The four of us squeezed into the cab. Miss Arlene handed me her cane. I laid it across my lap, gripping it like the safety bar of a roller coaster. Clemmie did the same. Thad sat by the door, white-knuckled and twitching.

"Arliss always drove this mechanical beast. I guess I'd better get comfortable with it." She gave me a weak smile.

"Yes, ma'am." I prayed we wouldn't meet any cars, animals, potted plants, or people on the road.

She cranked the ignition and King Kong roared to life. It belched a cloud of black smoke and promptly died.

Thad reached for the door handle. "Well, we tried."

Clemmie yanked him back.

Miss Arlene turned the key again and this time King Kong stayed running. Thad groaned and huddled against the door when we set off, lurching and bouncing our way down Pembroke Avenue, claiming only the life of the large trash can outside Heather Dawn's coffee shop.

I put a hand on the dashboard of King Kong in a feeble attempt to stabilize myself. Clemmie focused straight ahead, and Thad lost more color. I figured if I could distract him, maybe he'd remember to inhale. Plus, aside from the library, the next best way to learn about Eudora and Gifton was sitting right next to me.

"So, Miss Arlene, you knew Koo—I mean, Miss Klinch when you were younger, right? I know she was a historian, but what was she like?"

Miss Arlene thought for a while.

"She was an only child and she never married—always so focused on her work—but she was as sharp as Vermont cheddar. Trying to sneak something past her was like trying to sneak a sunrise past a rooster."

Clemmie straightened. "Are we talking about the same person, Miss Arlene?"

Good question. The young Miss Klinch sounded nothing like the muttering old lady replanting cemetery flowers in her yard.

Miss Arlene blew through a stop sign.

"Philip Johnson!" Thad squeezed his eyes shut. "Ma'am, you sure you have the right glasses on?"

"Oh, thank you, Thad." With both hands, she fumbled for the pair lost in her silver coils.

I grabbed the wheel as Clemmie swore under her breath. Miss Arlene plucked off the pair she wore and replaced them with the new ones from on top of her head.

"Much better." She grinned. "What else? Let's see. Eudora played the piano for quite a few years, and she was the curator at the Georgia Coastal Museum over in... Oh, where was it?" She tapped the steering wheel. "Savannah? Brunswick? One of those big cities on the coast."

"What's a curator?" Thad asked, eyes still squeezed shut.

"Someone who's in charge of a museum," Clemmie explained.

Miss Arlene nodded. "That's right. They choose and care for the museum's collections, like Muggie Shore does for our little museum. Even though Eudora worked elsewhere, she lived here and knew everything about our town's history."

The engine moaned. So did Thad.

"Don't worry," Clemmie whispered to him. "We're almost there."

"I think you might want to switch gears, Miss Arlene," I suggested.

"Good idea." She stomped on the clutch, jerked the gearshift into my knee, and then shoved it forward. The groaning stopped. Unfortunately, so did King Kong. "Oh dear. I must've let up on the clutch too quickly." Miss Arlene restarted the truck and we lurched forward. Her head bobbed as the truck juddered and shuddered down the road.

"I've never seen the inside of her house before," I said, "only the outside."

"Well, you're in for a sight." Miss Arlene grinned. "The place is over a hundred years old and so is most of what's inside. Normally these old family homes are passed down to the next of kin 'as is,' and they are full of possessions relatives don't want but can't throw out because of the emotional connection." She seemed to have recovered from yesterday's news about Badger and talked as fast as an auctioneer on caffeine. "Eudora used to bring in the most beautiful antiques to the Music Box—before her mind went. After that, she brought us a watermelon and box of Tupperware lids."

For the thousandth time I wished Kooky Klinch had been a normal relative and left the place to Dad and me. We wouldn't have cared about its condition or the extra junk and furniture. Heck—we'd *want* the stuff if we were going to live in a place that big. Or sell it to pay off our debts.

As if she'd read my thoughts, Miss Arlene spoke. "Don't take it personally Eudora didn't leave y'all the house. A first cousin twice removed is pretty distant. She didn't know you were her family any more than you knew she was yours. When people live alone all their lives and don't know their relatives, they usually share with organizations that meant the most to them. She obviously loved cats and wanted them cared for."

Even though that was true, her words didn't make me feel any better.

King Kong, courtesy of Miss Arlene, took out a fence post and I learned the name of one more architect, Antoni Gaudí.

CHAPTER 21

EUDORA KLINCH'S MANSION CROWNED a small hill.

Maybe it wasn't a mansion, but with its turrets and huge wraparound front porch, it looked like one. Plus, it was way bigger than our mobile home. Even though more dirt than paint clung to the exterior, and a couple shutters hung catawampus, it was obvious Eudora's collection of homeless cats had a place so much nicer than Dad and me.

And soon *we'd* need shelter.

Thad leaned forward, wide-eyed. "Look at the gabled roof and that woodwork. Classic Victorian."

Clemmie and I exchanged knowing glances. He'd be fine now.

At the peak of the long, sloping driveway sat a bright-red

Harley-Davidson motorcycle with a sidecar. A matching helmet rested on the seat. I figured it must belong to the person from the Tipton County Cat Society. No way had it belonged to Eudora.

We parked alongside the motorcycle. Clemmie and Thad hustled out before King Kong's engine shut off. Miss Arlene opened the latch on her purse and dropped the keys inside, then turned to me.

"Remember what I said yesterday about that glass being refillable, Grady?" she said.

"Yes, ma'am."

She exhaled. "Today I feel like I'm either filling that glass with a fire hose or an eyedropper."

"Yes, ma'am. I know what you mean. Water pressure can be almost as difficult to figure out as girls."

She chuckled and opened her door, and then turned to me. "You're a good listener and you make me laugh." She slid down from her seat and I handed her the cane. I wiggled out of my backpack, left it on the seat, and got out the opposite door to join Clemmie and Thad.

All four of us made our way toward the porch. The morning air already held the uncomfortable kind of heat that only broke with a storm. I glanced up. Clumps of swollen gray clouds gathered in the distance. No doubt they'd break open before the day ended.

A short woman in rolled-up jeans, tennis shoes, and a Texas

Rangers baseball cap opened the front door and stepped out, letting the screen door slam behind her. She held a gas-station coffee cup in one hand and waved with the other.

Thad grabbed my wrist and pulled me back. "Dude," he whispered. "A Rangers fan? I don't know about this."

I wriggled my hand away. Thad didn't trust anyone who didn't idolize the Braves.

"Arlene, good of you to come on such short notice." The Rangers fan moved way faster than Miss Arlene, and looked younger, with blond streaks in her ponytail that stuck out from under her ball cap.

"Nonsense, Teta Lynne." Miss Arlene swished her hand dismissively. "I was thrilled you called." She planted her cane at the base of the steps and rested her hands on top of each other. "Just yesterday, I was telling my assistants here that I needed to replace the items that got damaged when, when..." She pulled a hankie from her pocket and dabbed at the corners of her eyes. "God rest Arliss's soul."

"I'm so sorry for your loss." Teta Lynne squeezed Arlene's hand and then smiled at us. "You're the assistants then?"

Miss Arlene pointed her cane at us. "Thaddeus, Clementine, and Grady." She shoved her hankie back inside her pocket. "They'll help pack and carry the items to the truck. This is Mrs. Greene from—"

Teta Lynne's hand shot up. "Call me Teta Lynne, and don't think about adding a 'Miss' or 'ma'am.' I'm not in the mood." She winked. "Come on in and take a look-see." She opened the door but kept talking. "Everything is pretty much how we found it, although I did clean out the refrigerator. The society thought it best to sell the house and put all the proceeds toward a brand-new animal shelter." She threw a grin over her shoulder. "Exciting, right? Y'all love animals, don't you?" She moved inside without waiting for us to answer.

I couldn't look her in the eye. I wasn't loving those cats and their big house at the moment.

And good luck selling this place. The real estate market was slow right now, according to Dad. No one had bought our place. Of course, who wanted a run-down mobile home? Two years ago, I sure didn't.

Now I'd do anything to stay.

We followed her into a large entry hall.

"Gracious me," Miss Arlene said, yanking her hankie out once more and shielding her nose.

This time I reckoned her watery eyes weren't due to memories of Arliss. The air smelled bad enough to gag a maggot.

Teta Lynne acknowledged our dismayed faces. "Trust me, *this* is an improvement."

Miss Arlene had been spot-on when she said we were in for

a sight—but she failed to mention we were also in for a smell. The air reeked of cat pee even though Teta Lynne had the windows open and fans on. She'd even hung pine-scented air fresheners from anything with a ledge or a hook, but my nose still burned with the ammonia stench.

"Does it smell this bad because no one was here to take care of the cats after she died?" Clemmie asked.

Teta Lynne shook her head. "No. Sadly, the house was in this condition while Eudora was still alive. As soon as we got word she'd passed, we came and got the cats. Most have already been adopted." She lit a candle and waved the match through the air. "Sometimes people have too many pets and aren't able to properly care for them. I'm sure Eudora meant well taking in all those strays, but as you can see, or rather smell, it was more than one person could handle."

"No wonder she was always digging up the outdoors with her shovel," Thad muttered. "She was probably getting some fresh air."

"With new paint and carpet, the smell should be gone," said Teta Lynne. "The painters come tomorrow and the carpet a couple days after that, which is why anything you want has to go today. The rest is dumpster and thrift store bound."

A wide wooden staircase led up from the middle of the entry hall to the second floor. The living room extended to my left, and some kind of sitting room was on the right. A grandfather clock older than dirt moaned an off-key 8:30 a.m. melody.

Teta Lynne frowned at the clock and handed Miss Arlene a stack of lime-green sticky notes. "Slap these on things you want. Feel free to take that clock and put it out of its misery. The only thing not up for grabs is my motorcycle." She chuckled.

"That's yours?" Miss Arlene asked.

"Sure is."

"I bet it corners smoother than King Kong," Clemmie said.

"*Anything* corners smoother than King Kong," Thad muttered.

"I've wanted one for years and finally got that one last month," Teta Lynne said. "Candy-apple red too. My dog, Peachy-Pooh usually sits in the sidecar, but I didn't think it'd be wise to bring her today."

"Not unless Peachy-Pooh loves cats," Thad said.

"Arlene, let me give you a quick tour," Teta Lynne said. "And then you can take your time tagging what you want." She pointed at us and added, "After that the three musketeers can pack and load, and you and I will take my bike out for a spin. I've got a spare helmet."

Miss Arlene's eyes lit up. "Deal." She turned and handed Clemmie, Thad, and me each our own stack of notes. "Look around. If you see something you think might be good for the

Music Box, stick one of these on it. I'll check and decide when I get to that room." She hobbled through to the parlor with Teta Lynne.

Thad fanned at the air and leaned toward Clemmie and me. "I can't say I blame Miss Arlene for wanting to get out in the fresh air, but should she be getting on a motorcycle?"

"She'll be fine," Clemmie said. "I'm sure Teta Lynne will go slow."

I checked to be sure they were out of earshot. "Let's start looking for anything that might help us find the treasure."

"Like what?" Clemmie asked.

"Eudora was a historian, so, she probably had a lot of books and notes and stuff." I poked my head into the living room and scanned the furnishings for bookcases, but there weren't any.

Clemmie said, "I keep all my books in my room. Maybe she did too. Let's explore upstairs." She rested her hand on the banister.

CHAPTER 22

WE HURRIED UP THE wide staircase to the second-story landing. A hallway stretched in both directions, with lots of doors on each side. Another narrower staircase was tucked at the end of the hall. Thankfully the smell of urine wasn't as strong upstairs. Maybe the cats preferred the first floor.

"Let's split up," I said. "I'm not really sure what we're looking for, but holler if you find anything interesting. Maybe Teta Lynne will let us keep it. She doesn't want the stuff anyway."

Thaddeus pointed to the other set of stairs. "Architecturally speaking, those stairs probably lead to servants' quarters and the attic."

"Cool," Clemmie said. "Let's go—I want to check out the tower-looking things."

"Turrets," he corrected as she dragged him down the hall.

"I'll start here," I said to the empty hallway.

The first bedroom didn't look like the master. The brass bed had a threadbare patchwork quilt. Two dirty windows framed an old dresser, and a rocking chair crouched in the corner. I opened the windows to air the space out. When I discovered all the dresser drawers were empty, I slapped a sticky note on the brass part of the bed and left.

The next two rooms offered the same disappointing results with old furniture but no personal belongings.

Same for the rooms on the other side of the hall. Frustration knotted my gut. Nothing but dust and the smell of cat urine. The last room was much larger and had more windows and a bigger bed across from a dresser. A squishy-looking armchair perched between bookcases. But no books. No framed pictures or jewelry, no surface clutter at all. Only dust and cat hair.

I yanked open the dresser drawers. Empty.

There were no clothes hanging in the closet.

No towels in the bathroom.

Nor a toothbrush or toothpaste or bar of soap.

Back in the hallway I ran into Clemmie. Thad stood behind her, shifting his weight back and forth.

"These rooms are pretty much empty," I grumped.

Thad nodded. "Same with the ones we checked. Not even

toilet paper in the bathroom, which is *really* disappointing 'cause I gotta go."

We headed toward the stairs.

"It's so weird," Clemmie said. "Why have all this space if you don't use it?"

The floors creaked when Teta Lynne and Miss Arlene climbed the steps and joined us on the landing.

"Muggie Shore told me Eudora stopped using the top floor ages ago," Teta Lynne said. "The stairs became too much of a challenge, and she was afraid she'd fall. This was before she started—" She paused, clearly searching for the right words.

"Going kooky?" Thad said.

"Before she lost her grip on reality," Teta Lynne corrected. "About ten years ago she called up Muggie and said she wanted to donate several items to the Gifton museum but needed help getting them there. So, Muggie and the mayor helped her move her personal belongings downstairs—clothes, photographs, anything she wanted to keep—and took the rest to the museum."

"What about her books? Are they downstairs?" I asked, with a feather-like flutter of hope in my chest. Maybe they were somewhere we hadn't explored yet.

Teta Lynne tapped her finger on her chin. "Hmm. Can't say I've seen any. She might have donated all of them. Check with Muggie."

"Thanks." I turned to Miss Arlene. "I marked some things for you. There wasn't much."

"Same with us," Thad said.

"Thank you, dears." She lifted her much thinner stack of sticky notes. "I've slapped these on several items downstairs if y'all want to start packing and loading. There's a whole bunch of hand-painted china that will need to be wrapped in newspaper before boxing it."

"Teta Lynne, where's the bathroom?" asked Thad.

"First floor, turn left at the bottom of the stairs, second door on the right."

He raced downstairs, and Clemmie and I hurried behind. Just because we found nothing upstairs didn't mean there wasn't *something* downstairs that could still help us find the treasure. Thad spun left, while Clemmie and I turned right toward the living room.

Despite the thick layer of dust and cat hair on most surfaces, Miss Arlene had tagged furniture, knickknacks, picture frames, and more. At first glance, everything looked normal. *Un*-kooky. Furniture sat in rooms, pictures hung on walls, and magazines sat stacked on the entryway table. Nothing like what I pictured for Kooky Klinch.

But peculiar things became noticeable—handwritten notes everywhere. On index cards and scraps of paper, even grocery store receipts. Strange notes. Like the one stuck to the kitchen fridge with a magnet: *Put oatmeal in a bowl, not in bedroom slippers.*

Or the one on top of the side table near the sofa: *Green is your favorite color.*

I moved around looking for more. One was taped to the wall beside the front door: *Your address is 723 Sweet Moss Drive.*

On the piano was one that said: *You love Beethoven and Gershwin, but not Chopin.*

I liked Gershwin too. His piece, *An American in Paris* was my favorite. At least Eudora and I had something in common even if Dad and I didn't.

Another near the fireplace read: *Neurology appointment, Atlanta, March 7th at 3:35pm. Don't forget this time.*

So Kooky Klinch must've had dementia or Alzheimer's or some other terrible memory condition.

I walked back through every room, collecting the notes.

Teta Lynne rambled into the room and looked at the pile in my hands. "Just leave them, hon. They'll get tossed with everything else."

I shoved them in my pocket. "They seem like her last words. Hardly seems right to just throw them away."

Teta Lynne cocked her head. "You know what, you're right."

Teta Lynne tucked Miss Arlene into the motorcycle's sidecar.

"If you are done packing before we get back, you can load

the boxes into the truck," Miss Arlene said. "Just leave the furniture. It's too heavy. Teta Lynne is taking me by Clymer's place. He'll come with Charlie and get that grandfather clock and the rest of the big stuff." And off they went, toodling down the road, Miss Arlene laughing in the sidecar of the candy-apple-red motorcycle.

In the living room Clemmie found one of Eudora's memory cards I'd missed from my earlier sweep. "*E left, then E. Pembroke. The library!*" she read. "What's that supposed to mean?"

Thad wrapped a teacup in newspaper and settled it in the box on the table in front of him. He thought for a moment. "Probably directions to the library. It's on East Pembroke Avenue. But not a very direct route from her house."

"I wish she'd left directions to the treasure instead," Clemmie said. "That'd make things a lot easier." She set the card down and walked over to help Thad pack the delicate dishes.

"I still don't get how I could've been so wrong about the church," I said. "Everything seemed to fit the riddle perfectly."

"Explain it again," Clemmie said.

I knew the words as well as I knew my birthday. "'Seek ye first the Kingdom of God, stay close to all ye held dear. Three layers of stone and one of timber, that which ye seeks is here,'" I said.

"Maybe you overthought it," she said. "There have to be other places around here made with stone layers and wood."

I puffed out my cheeks. "Probably. Did y'all bring your phones?"

"I did," Thad said, "but the battery died on the way over— kinda like we almost did."

Clemmie rolled her eyes and handed me hers.

"Thanks." I plopped down on the sofa and a cloud of cat hair puffed into the air.

Clemmie brought newspapers and plates to the coffee table and sat next to me. "What are you searching?"

"Seeing if there's a map of colonial Gifton. It'd be dumb to keep looking in places if they didn't even exist when Elizabeth was alive. I'm not making that mistake again."

No map of colonial Gifton appeared on the screen. I flopped against the back of the sofa. "We've got to get to the museum. I bet it has a map. Plus, with so many of Miss Klinch's things there, something there could help us figure out the riddle. I've been there a few times, but I've never really paid much attention to the stuff on the walls. I like looking at the artifacts more than reading old love letters."

Clemmie shoved a pile of newspaper my way. "Well, get busy. The sooner we pack up all this junk, the sooner we can get out of here. Maybe go to the museum."

"Yeah, yeah." I tossed her phone to her, took the newspaper, and headed over to the piano, which was covered with knickknacks we needed to wrap. I picked up the memory card Clemmie had laid down—the one with the directions to the library. I shoved it into my back pocket with the others. "She had Alzheimer's or something."

"It would explain the notes," Clemmie said. "That's sad."

Thad slumped his shoulders. "I thought she was just a bit odd. I didn't realize she was really losing her mind. I feel bad for making fun of her and calling her kooky."

"Me too." I started wrapping a glass figure of a parrot. "Race you," I said to Thad. "Bet I can wrap all this junk on top of the piano before you finish those teacups."

"Boys. Boys. Don't be breaking things," Clemmie said.

A few minutes later I dropped the last knickknack into my box. "I won."

Thad still had eight cups left.

I lifted the piano bench lid. Lots of Beethoven and Gershwin music books, and not a single piece by Chopin. I flipped through the music and stopped at the score to *An American in Paris*. "Is Miss Arlene taking these?"

"I heard her tell Teta Lynne that she couldn't move the piano and they don't sell well, anyway," Thad said.

"I mean the music books."

"Is there a sticky note on them?" Clemmie asked.

"Just on the stuff on top of the piano."

"Then I guess she's not taking them."

What Miss Arlene said about old homes being full of stuff relatives couldn't throw away because they were "emotionally connected" to them wasn't true in Eudora's case. No one was connected. Most of her stuff would be tossed into the dumpster and forgotten.

I wasn't going to let that happen.

I would remember her.

There'd be no room in the camper for anything big, but Gershwin would fit in the ammo box—along with the sampler and my other special items, once I got it back from Clemmie.

I picked up the piano book, took Eudora's notes from my pocket, and stashed them inside the pages. "I'll be right back." Holding the book, I dashed out to King Kong and shoved it all in my backpack.

The grandfather clock in the hall moaned ten wheezing strokes when I walked back inside the living room. "Let's finish collecting everything Miss Arlene wanted and load the truck. When they get back, we can leave right away. Then we can go to the museum and talk to Muggie."

"Maybe we can go there after lunch," Thad said.

"As long as we go today." I grabbed a box. "Dad said we have to start packing up the house in two days. I won't have time for treasure hunting after that."

Clemmie breathed in sharply.

The room got quiet, but I pretended not to notice—just headed to the truck with my box.

We were just about done loading the van when Miss Arlene came back. She was laughing as she crawled out of the sidecar. It looked like the motorcycle ride had made her forget Arliss for a bit.

"Wow!" she said. "You kids have been working!"

We made it back to town, and thanks to Miss Arlene's driving, I learned the names of three new architects, Mies van der Rohe, Jeanne Gang, and Zaha Hadid.

CHAPTER 23

MISS ARLENE PARKED KING Kong in front of the Music Box. Sort of. She opened her door and walked around the front of the truck while Clemmie, Thad, and I tumbled out our side.

Deputy Oringderff, who stood nearby, raised her brow. "Creative parking job, Arlene."

She smiled. "Oh, thank you."

Deputy Oringderff cleared her throat. "I need to ask you a few more questions, but before I do, how about I straighten out King Kong—or at least remove him from blocking the fire hydrant on the sidewalk."

Miss Arlene dropped the keys in the deputy's outstretched hand. "That'd be lovely." She turned to us. "Just put the boxes in the back room and you can take the rest of the day off. No need to unpack. I want to go through and research some of these items before I price them and put them out in the store."

It took us about twenty minutes to unload. Then we hurried across Pembroke Avenue to the courthouse library. Clemmie and I sprinted up to the front door.

"Guys, wait," Thad called.

I turned, surprised to see him at the bottom of the steps. "What's wrong?"

He glanced around like he was making sure no one else was listening and then waved us back down. "I was just thinking if whoever broke into the Music Box finds out we're poking around and asking questions about Miss Klinch and the War of Jenkins's Ear"—he lowered his voice even more—"there could be...more trouble."

"Don't worry," I said. "I switched samplers, remember? Whoever the thief is has Mama's replica from the Civil War."

"Yeah," Clemmie said. "They'll be thinking the treasure has something to do with that. No one's gonna care if we're researching colonial stuff."

"Oh yeah. Good point," he said. "I forgot about that."

"We should split up since we have a lot of ground to cover and not a lot of time." Clemmie turned to me. "You and Thad ask Muggie about the items from Eudora's house. Explain that when we were helping Miss Arlene, we talked about history and wanted to see what she donated. Nothing strange about that—especially since Thad's always messing around in old buildings and everyone knows you're trying to learn about your long-lost relative."

"Who put you in charge?" Thad asked.

She ignored him. "I'll see what's on the walls besides old letters, diary entries, and stuff. Maybe there's a map or poster about the original colony." She held up her phone. "And I'll take pictures so we can look at everything later."

"Agreed," I said.

Thad faced me. "You're only agreeing because it's easier than arguing with her."

"Agreed," I repeated. "But we'll have to be sneaky. Muggie had a fit last time she caught someone taking photos. Hollered about how the light from the flash would damage the artifacts."

"I'm the Queen of Sneaky." Clemmie grinned and bounded up the steps into the library. We followed and continued to the second-floor museum.

I nudged Clemmie. "We need those photos, so be careful. We'll distract her, but hurry."

She nodded and veered to the right as soon as we walked through the doorway.

The heat of the day made the old courthouse's brand-new air-conditioning a welcome break, but we weren't the only folks in Gifton who felt that way. People milled around the wood-paneled room, glancing in the glass cases and cabinets filled near to overflowing.

Most of the displays held really cool things like arrowheads and Civil War weaponry—one even had bone fragments. Muggie claimed for years they belonged to her late relative, General Holliston Foles, who she considered to be a Civil War hero. Apparently his finger was shot clean off by a misbehaving cannon. Deputy Oringderff swore they were squirrel bones. I was inclined to believe the deputy seeing how if a cannon misfired, the general would've lost a lot more than just a finger.

Muggie stood by an opened case wearing something like a carpenter's apron. A ruler and feather duster sprouted out of one of the pockets. A pale-blue scarf was tied in a floppy bow around her neck. She faced our direction and held a thin object in one white-gloved hand and a polishing cloth in the other. During our field trip to the museum last year, she explained her gloves protected the artifacts from the oils on her hands.

Thad leaned toward me. "She looks like an old-fashioned airline attendant with her scarf and gloves."

I wouldn't know.

We hurried past a couple visitors. "Follow me," I whispered, circling behind so she'd have to turn to talk to us.

"Hi, Muggie," I said.

She spun and smiled. "Hello, Grady. Hello, Thad." Between her thumb and finger, she pinched an old, dented metal fork. She stopped polishing. "How are y'all this afternoon?"

"Fine, ma'am, thanks," I said. "I have a question for you about Miss Eudora."

She cocked her head. "What's your question?" She held the fork toward the light, gave a nod of approval, replaced it in the case, and picked up the spoon next to it.

I tried to calm the fluttering in my chest with a deep breath. Finding something...*anything* among Eudora's donations was my only hope at this point. "Earlier today we were helping Miss Arlene pack up some of Miss Klinch's things and found out she'd donated a bunch of stuff to the museum." I fidgeted. "Ever since I heard she was a relative, I've been, umm, trying to...learn as much as I can about her."

"That's completely understandable, dear. Family's important." She glanced into the case, set the feather duster down, and adjusted the location of the fork ever so slightly.

Clemmie moved silently from one wall display to the next, taking photos.

"Can we see what she donated?" I asked.

Muggie replaced the spoon, closed the glass lid, and grabbed her feather duster. "Well now, it was many years ago. There were several boxes and pieces of furniture." She tugged at her gloves and opened the next case. "If the items were artifacts, they're up here in the museum."

"What kind of artifacts?" I asked.

Muggie ran the duster over a row of Civil War buttons. "Things like oil lamps, some vintage jewelry, a pocket watch." She pointed to a table at the far end of the room. "That model ship of the *Mirage* was hers. It's one our most prized possessions, aside from General Foles's remains, or what's left of him—may he rest in peace."

"Rest in pieces is more like it," muttered Thad.

Clemmie stopped in front of a sign on the wall above Eudora's donated model ship. She stood directly in Muggie's line of sight.

Thad must've noticed too, because he quickly moved several feet to the right and pointed at a random object in the case. "What about this, uh"—he looked down—"pipe? Was this part of her stuff?"

Muggie joined him and peered through the glass. "Hmmm. I don't think so, love, but it's hard to be sure since it was many years ago." She screwed her face in thought. "There were a few furniture pieces that I added to our 1800s domestic life exhibit." She gestured toward the front of the museum where a butter churn, a spinning wheel, a rickety table holding an oil lamp, a whole bunch of pots and pans, and a fire extinguisher took up one corner.

"Oh dear, I forgot to light the lamp." She hurried over.

Thad and I followed.

Muggie whipped out a lighter from her apron and flicked it open. A flame sprang to life and remained dancing.

Thad's mouth dropped. "You keep a lighter?"

Muggie chuckled. "It was my grandfather's. This apron is like a wearable emergency kit. I keep all sorts of items in here— and good thing too. A couple weeks ago I changed this display from early colonial to mid-1800s, and I keep forgetting to light this lamp." She lit the wick, but the flame fizzled out almost immediately. She lifted the lamp and examined the base. "Oh drat. The wick is too short to reach the oil. Oh well. I'll change it out later." She sighed, dropped the lighter back into her pocket, and meandered back to the display of Civil War buttons.

From the large windows behind her, the tops of the oak trees swayed, and clouds stacked on top of each other. One way or another, the humidity was going to break.

"So did Eudora Klinch donate any books?" I asked.

"Hang on a minute, love." She squatted eye level next to the buttons and scrutinized them. Then she stood, whipped out a ruler, and laid it beside the buttons. She scowled and finger-tapped the one on the far left twice. Like I said, she could be particular.

Apparently satisfied with the result, she dropped the ruler into her apron pocket and shut the case lid. "I sent the books down to Miss Cornett. I figured they'd be better utilized in the library."

I wasn't holding my breath. Miss Cornett already told me the library didn't have anything on Elizabeth Radcliffe. Clemmie gave us a thumbs-up and waved us over.

"Thanks, Muggie." I tugged on Thad's arm. "We'll check out the library later." I dragged him with me over to where Clemmie stood. "Did you get pictures of everything?"

"Yes, and I have good news and bad news. Which do you want first?"

"It's always better to get the bad news over with," Thad said.

"Follow me." She led us to a large, framed sketch of a church that sort of looked like a one-room schoolhouse with a bell tower. "The original church was tabby stone and wood."

"That's good. We need stone and wood," I said.

Clemmie grimaced. "Yeah—but we need *three* layers of stone, and according to this description, there were only two. The foundation and the outer walls. The roof was wood."

"But the walls would've been made from several layers of tabby stone, right?" I asked. "We just have to count two layers up from the foundation."

Thad shook his head. "The walls were made of multiple layers, yes, but once complete, they'd have been covered in stucco and painted. It would look like one solid layer."

My shoulders dropped. "If there are only two layers, the treasure's definitely not there. Quick. Tell me the good news."

She looked around like she was making sure no one was watching us and then wiggled one finger to get us to follow her. "Let's go back to the model ship." She pointed where to a framed poster titled *How Gifton Got Its Name* hung on the wall. "Check this out!"

Thad groaned. "I have to read all that?"

Clemmie rolled her eyes. "Don't be such a baby. It basically says a long time ago, ships like the *Mirage* loaded their hulls with heavy objects called 'ballast.' Stuff like rocks, sandbags, and even extra cannons."

"Why?" I asked.

"The weight kept the ships from capsizing. When they got to America, the ballast would be thrown overboard and—"

"Even the cannons?" Thad asked.

"No doofus, not the cannons," she said. "The rocks and sand. Then natural resources like timber would be loaded in their place and taken back to England." She pointed to the poster. "This says Gifton's first settlers asked the captain if they could keep a ballast stone to remember England by. He gave them the largest one and—"

"I would've asked for a cannon," Thad muttered.

"Quit interrupting," Clemmie said.

"I'm confused," I said. "What does this have to do with the treasure?"

She huffed and pointed to a section. "Just read starting here."

The colonists later formed a monument, using the beloved gift of the ballast stone. Tabby stone, the local building material, formed the base and symbolized their new start in a new land. The ballast stone was placed on the base, and then another layer of tabby stone crowned the top. The man-made monument (which many people think resembles a piece of candy corn) embodied the idea that while England would always be in the center of their hearts, their new home (filled with mosquitoes and overbearing humidity) was now in Georgia.

"Why would they want to remember England?" asked Thad. "I thought they were happy to leave."

"Not everybody," I said. "Lots of people left behind family they'd never see again."

"Keep reading," Clemmie urged.

A wooden cross, reminding the settlers of their

religious freedom, capped the three-foot-tall structure that is still located on the edge of town. (Due to the hurricane of 1898, the cross is no longer there. If found, please return it to the museum).

"Not everyone had religious freedom though," Thad said. "I remember that much of history at least."

I nodded. "Yeah. Mrs. Maragos said Catholics weren't allowed to live there, because the British governor thought they'd side with Spain since Spain was Catholic."

"Stay focused." Clemmie tapped the poster.

At first, the settlement was called Giftstone, harkening back to the captain's gift of a ballast stone. Over time, it was shortened to Gifton, which was much easier to say. (While the monument would make a great addition in the museum, it's too heavy to move, let alone haul up multiple flights of stairs. Feel free to visit it near mile marker 105.)

Clemmie whispered, her dark eyes bright with excitement. "You see it, right? Pretty wild, huh?"

"Calling that blob of rock a monument *is* wild," Thad said. "That's a stretch."

Clemmie stared at him. "No, dork brain. I'm talking about the riddle."

I could hardly stand still. I was ready to go right then and there and find the monument. "There's *three layers* of stone. And the wooden cross is the timber layer. That's it."

Thad let out a low whistle.

"Everything fits," Clemmie said. "The layers, the Kingdom of God reference with the cross, even the timing. The stone would've been there when Elizabeth was alive. And that part about staying close to what you hold dear could mean maybe they loved England and the stone reminded them of that. I don't know, but—" She grabbed my arm. "Grady, the treasure has to be hidden *under* that monument at the edge of town."

"Clemmie, you're a genius." I looked out the windows. The clouds were closer and darker, but maybe we could make it. "Come on. We have time to dig. Let's go!"

CHAPTER 24

THAD AND I GOT the two shovels at his house while Clemmie ran down the street and got another from her garage. I'd biked past the monument a thousand times and never paid any attention to it. Now, the man-made boulder and the riddle were the only things I focused on as I balanced the shovel across my handlebars and raced alongside Clemmie and Thad. *Seek ye first the Kingdome of God. Stay close to all ye held dear. Three layers of stone and one of timbre. That which ye seeks is hear.*

When we got to mile marker 105 on the edge of town, next to Mayor Shore's WELCOME TO GIFTON sign, I dropped my bike in the dirt and rushed to the rock.

Clemmie skidded to a stop next to me. "It totally looks like a piece of candy corn."

She wasn't wrong.

The layered gray boulder was roughly triangular in shape, and just reached past my waist. Bits of oyster shell that had been mixed in with the tabby stone jutted out here and there. We'd have to be careful when we dug not to cut ourselves on them. I pointed to two small, rusted metal plates embedded on the top. "I bet the wooden cross was bolted to those before it blew off in the hurricane."

"Why does rain only come when we're about to dig?" asked Thad, glancing up at the black clouds in the sky and letting his bike fall next to mine.

"Seriously," Clemmie agreed.

I jammed my shovel into the clay. The blade sunk only a few inches. "Pick a spot and start digging."

"What if someone sees us?" Thad asked.

Clemmie scoffed. "Hardly anyone drives *into* Gifton. If anyone asks us what we're doing, we'll tell them it's a beautification project. We'll plant flowers in honor of Eudora Klinch when we're done to celebrate finding the treasure." She grinned at me. "We just won't take them from the cemetery."

"Works for me," I said. "Besides, it shouldn't take too long to dig. This is pretty small for a monument."

Thunder rumbled and leaves spun in a whirlwind at our feet. The storm was closer than it sounded as clouds skittered above us in a dark line.

"If we think digging's hard now," Clemmie said, "the rain will make it harder. Wet ground gets slippery, and clay weighs a ton."

For the second time in less than a week we dug.

And dug.

And dug.

Not a single car has passed us. No one saw the sweat running down my face. Or Thad's skin turning pink from the heat and the work. Or Clemmie, who in a quiet fit of frustration with her braids hanging in her face, pulled them back into a knot.

We dug all around the monument's base. Mounds of dirt lay scattered at our feet. At some point, I abandoned my shovel and scooped out chunks of clay and dirt with my hands. With each handful I shoved behind me, I grew more confident that the next would reveal the edge of a wooden chest or box.

The storm crept closer. Humidity increased. Sweat plastered our clothes on us.

The treasure had to be here *somewhere*.

"How far down you reckon we need to go?" Thad asked.

I wiped my shirtsleeve across my face to stop the sweat from stinging my eyes. "Till we find it."

"We'd better hurry then." Clemmie looked up at the large drops of water splattering the rock, the ground, and us.

The drops turned into sheets of water, making our trench a

muddy moat. I stayed on my knees at the base of the monument, pulling sludge from the hole as fast as it slogged in.

Thad stopped digging.

So did Clemmie.

"Grady." Thad leaned against his shovel. "The rock's not that big, and we've been here for a while. We're two feet down using good strong shovels. Elizabeth wouldn't have been able to even go this far." Raindrops fell from his hair. "It was a good idea, but the treasure's not here."

"Quit if you want," I snapped. "I'm staying. I'm not going home." Soon I wouldn't have a home to go to.

My back was to them but I *knew* they were looking at each other. Lightning ripped through the clouds. Thunder shook the ground.

"Grady, we're leaving." Clemmie pulled firmly on my arm. "All of us. It's not safe out here. We'll try again tomorrow if you want. Move it. Now!"

I spun on my knees in the mud. We were all soaked. More lightning lit up the sky. The wind pummeled the WELCOME TO GIFTON sign, splattering it with leaves.

Thad grabbed my shovel with one hand and held his in the other. "Dude. We're not going to find the treasure if we get struck by lightning."

Groaning, I stood and trudged to my bike. "Where else

could it be? This is impossible! No wonder Miss Klinch lost her mind." I yanked the bike up and straddled the seat. "I hate this!"

"I know. I'm sorry," Clemmie said, before pushing off on her bike.

Thad handed me a shovel. "Come on. We've got to get out—" His words were drowned out by crashing thunder.

We raced against the wind and rain. When I got home, I dashed inside to get clean before Dad saw me and started asking questions. I showered with my clothes on to wash all the mud off. Then I wrung them out and watched the water swirl down the drain...taking my hope with it.

~~~

"Only pack what you'll need on a day-to-day basis," Dad said. "There won't be room for other stuff."

I peeled apart my peanut butter sandwich, hoping for jelly. None. I stuck the pieces back together and stared at Dad. At least we had dinner.

He picked up his sandwich. "The Carltons said we can store some boxes in their garage until we're...back on our feet."

"Why can't we stay in Gifton? We can live in Clymer Hine's camper here. Why do we have to go to Anaston?"

"There's not enough work here. I need a bigger city." He

pushed his plate away. "I'm sorry, Grady. I'll work it out though. You'll see."

I picked up my sandwich. "I'll be in my room." I grabbed an empty box with my free hand and slouched down the hall. I threw the box onto my bed and shut the door. "Emily Dickinson didn't know what she was talking about. Stupid hope with feathers."

The rain had stopped and had brought a drop in temperature. I decided to open my window to cool off, but before I reached it, Clemmie tapped on the glass and waved a folder.

I opened the window. "What are you doing here?"

"Were you talking to yourself just now?"

"Sort of," I said. "Just muttering about Emily Dickinson."

"The poet? Why?"

I shook my head. "It's stupid. What's that?" I pointed to the folder in her hand.

She handed the file to me. "All the pictures from the museum. I wanted to get them to you tonight, because Mama says I have to go with her into Anaston tomorrow. I took pictures of letters, diary entries, the posters on the walls. I enlarged them so they should be easy to read. Maybe there's something helpful." She climbed over the ledge of my window to the inside. "Some doctors think she probably suffered from a bipolar disorder. Emily Dickinson, I mean." She sat on the sill.

"Really? How do you know?" I set the folder on my bed next to the cardboard box.

"Dad told me."

How could a poem about hope perching in our souls and freeing us from despair and sadness have been written by someone who was trapped in despair and sadness herself? Or... maybe her struggles with depression *made her* the perfect person to write the poem. "Does your dad think she was depressed?"

"Yeah. Lots of psychiatrists these days do actually. He even has a lecture about it." She picked at a hole in her jean shorts. "She'd have these really dark times—usually during winter—but hey, who doesn't? Then she'd get really happy. Some people say she did her best writing during those 'dark' moments, so I guess maybe good came out of it." She shrugged. "I don't know. Feeling depressed probably sucked."

I wondered how long Emily Dickinson watched birds and thought about hope before reaching for her pen and paper. And why a bird? They're weird. They molt and lose all their feathers.

Not just once.

Lots of times.

You're staring at one ugly animal for a while until the feathers grow back.

But when they do, they are bigger.

And stronger.

Sometimes even a different color. I guess it's kind of like getting a brand-new bird.

Is that why she chose them for her poem? Is that what she meant when she wrote about hope being the thing with feathers? Maybe she felt her soul was ugly at times, and that she had no hope at that moment...but she knew the feathers would grow back? Maybe she believed her hope would return one day bigger and stronger than ever?

Dad and I seemed to be further apart than ever. New feathers didn't seem possible.

〜〜〜

Clemmie said good night and left through the window. I flipped the folder open. A letter from 1863 addressed to "My Dearest Samuel" from Katrina Gultch topped the pile. The first photos were of letters to and from Samuel and Katrina Gultch. I wanted to speed my search up, not read goopy love letters from the Civil War. I spread the rest of the photos across my mattress. There were a couple journal entries, a newspaper article from 1803 about a property dispute between neighbors, and a handful of recipes. And no idea why Muggie thought any of it was museum-worthy.

I skimmed the photo of the poster titled "Get to Know Gifton's Most Influential Citizens" and was about to set it aside when two names caught my attention.

Elizabeth. And then…*Radcliffe.*

I picked up the photo and read.

Nathaniel Pembroke (1724–1799)

- Born in Virginia
- Moved to Gifton as a widower in 1756, bringing with him an infant daughter.
- Wife: Elizabeth Pembroke, née Radcliffe (1734–1756). Died suddenly when thrown from her horse.
- Second wife: Rebecca Pembroke, née Flohre (1739–1792).
- Children: Annabelle (1756–1802, born to Elizabeth), Jonathan (1757–1792), Millicent (1759–1760), Simon (1763–1812), Marianne (1766–1825)
- Best known for: Highly successful farmer and district magistrate.
- He used his wealth to help support the militia during the American Revolution. Pembroke Avenue is named after him.

Née? What the heck did that mean? I flipped through the dictionary on my desk.

Née: Adjective. Originally called; born.

I swallowed my excitement as a thought exploded in my head. I jumped off the bed and rifled through my backpack. Eudora's memory notes were still inside the Gershwin music. I shuffled through them looking for one in particular. *E left, then E. Pembroke. The Library!*

Those weren't directions to the library at all. Eudora had learned Elizabeth Radcliffe had left Gifton, married, and became Elizabeth Pembroke—*E. left, then E. Pembroke*. The reason I couldn't find any information on Elizabeth Radcliffe earlier was because I was looking under the *wrong name*.

But what did the library part mean? Could it be that Eudora remembered there was something about the treasure in a book she'd donated? Was she reminding herself to go to the library and search?

I looked back at the photo. Nathaniel Pembroke moved to Gifton in 1756 as a widower—the same year that Elizabeth died. Maybe she told him about the treasure and that's why he moved here.

But Eudora had kept searching. She figured the treasure had never been found. I hoped she was right.

CHAPTER 25

SATURDAY MORNING, I GOT up early, figuring the odds of Dad letting me go to the library were better if I started packing my room. He'd said only take what could fit in one suitcase. I searched through the shirts on my side table but couldn't find my favorite green one. I checked the floor, and a familiar sleeve peeked from under my bed. When I tugged it out, along came a library book. Perfect.

I clutched the book and trotted down the hall. "Dad!"

"In the kitchen."

I set the book on the table. "Found this. I need to return it to the library."

He knelt on the floor near an open cabinet.

I cleared my throat. "I started packing." Maybe that would sway him to a yes.

He put a pot into the box next to him, looked at the book, and then the microwave clock. "Library doesn't open for another hour. Have some breakfast, help me pack a bit more, and then go."

I gritted my teeth. Darn! He was right. It was Saturday, and the library opened an hour later.

A box of Oatey-O's sat on the counter by my elbow. I poured myself a bowl and grabbed a spoon. We were out of milk. "Are you packing stuff we're taking with us to the camper or stuff that's going to Thad's garage?"

"Camper." He removed the medium-size pot from the box and replaced it with a smaller one. He gave me a weak smile. "It's a small kitchen."

"I bet," I muttered before shoving a spoonful of dry cereal into my mouth.

He rested his hands on his knees and pushed up. "Can I leave you to finish here? I've got to focus on the workshop." He scrubbed his hands over his bristly face quickly as though waking himself up.

"Sure." I eyed the library book. I had one hour to finish packing the kitchen.

~~~~

I slung my backpack onto my shoulders and raced to town. At the library, I dropped my bike under the elm tree closest to the flagpole, hurried up the steps, yanked open the door, and smacked right into Mayor Shore.

"Uff!" Mayor Shore wobbled backward but caught himself.

"I'm sorry, Mayor Shore." I picked up his fedora and handed it to him. "I didn't see you."

"Running that fast, I'm not surprised. Where's the fire, son?" He tucked his hat under an arm, tugged on his PRESS ball cap, and slid a small notebook out of his suit pocket.

"There's no fire, sir," I said.

His shoulders slumped. "Oh, that's too bad." With a sheepish look, he corrected himself. "Just something exciting would be nice for the paper is all," he said as he put his notebook away. "Muggie mentioned the museum might display a new artifact or two. Not sure how many people would consider that newsworthy." He leaned closer. "Don't tell her I said that."

I adjusted the backpack. "Uh, I—"

"Well, good day." He tipped his hat and left.

I returned my book and then had to hunt for Miss Cornett. I finally found her shelving books in the poetry section. "What does the library have on Elizabeth Pembroke?" I made a show of drumming my fingers nonchalantly on a shelf. "I'm, uh, doing a, um, book report." I stopped. "I mean, a summer book report on early Gifton settlers."

"That's certainly admirable." She wedged the last book into

place and motioned me to follow her to her desk. "Pembroke, you said? Let's check the computer." After some quick keyboard clicks, she nodded. "Looks like one of her diaries was donated by Eudora Klinch a few years ago. It's in the archival room though, and I don't normally allow anyone in there unsupervised." She checked her wristwatch. "I can't take you now. I have a meeting with the county library director in about ten minutes. But I'll take you after lunch."

I had to get home to pack. "My dad needs me to help him this afternoon. I can't come back after lunch. You can trust me, Miss Cornett."

"I don't know."

"I won't touch anything except the diary. And I'll—I'll shelve books for you later."

She gave me a squinty-eyed look. "Well, I *suppose* I could let you in there—but just to sit and read. Not that there's anything else *to* do. And there are certain rules you *have* to follow."

"I'll follow every rule, I promise."

"Come on."

I followed her down the main hall, around the corner, past the stairs leading up to the museum, and past the restrooms and the water fountain. Then we turned left into another long, dusty wood-paneled hallway. At the end of that hall, we turned to the right and kept going.

Finally, we stopped in front of a beat-up door, and she took keys from her pocket.

She let out a long sigh. "Our archival room is in rough shape, but the temperature and lighting are perfect for older documents. The light switch is on your right." Miss Cornett pointed to the wall.

I flicked the switch. "Why is the switch on the outside of the room?"

"*That* switch turns on the lights in the room next door as well. The electrical is wonkier than a rat maze. The good news is this entire wing is being remodeled."

She jammed the key into the lock and jiggled the knob. "We're emptying everything out of this room in the next couple of days, so you came at a good time." She gave the bottom of the door a couple hearty kicks and smiled apologetically as she shoved her shoulder against it.

The door opened into a dimly lit room with three small windows high up on the back wall. You could barely tell I'd turned the lights on, and if it was sunny outside, you couldn't tell by the gray light filtering through the grimy windows.

"When the building was still the courthouse, this room was originally a jail cell." Miss Cornett said. "That's why the windows sit so high. At least the bars aren't on them anymore. That'd make it even more depressing in here." She pointed to some shelves off to the left side of the room that were covered with painters' drop cloths or sheets or something. "These contain reference books, binders, and old papers. We're trying to keep them as clean as possible. Moving stuff for the remodel stirs up a lot of dust."

There were three aisles. Every few feet a file folder or notebook peeked out. None of the sheets were long enough. Dust covered the books on the exposed bottom shelves.

A pile of junk was near the back wall underneath the high windows. At least it looked like junk. Easels. A milk churn. An old washbasin. A grandfather clock. And other pieces of forgotten furniture.

There was another pile of stuff, covered with a dingy white sheet. A scuffed wooden bookcase stood nearby, holding a jumble of pitchers, plates, and enough empty oil lamps to light up Texas. "Sheesh."

Miss Cornett followed my gaze. "This room is meant for library archives, but the museum uses it for overflow. With the remodel, the museum gets its own storage area, which Muggie will love. She doesn't like anyone messing with her stuff. I try to stay out of her way. I offered to help her move things for the remodel, but she said no. You know how particular she can be. She'd have my head if she knew I was about to leave you here alone, so please don't mention it."

I nodded, then continued to look around the room.

Waist-high wooden storage cabinets with deep drawers lined

the right wall. Piles of old newspapers sat stacked here and there on top. A dust mop leaned against the set of drawers closest to me.

A couple feet away from the cabinets, in the middle of the room, under the dim, buzzing fluorescent light, sat a scuffed table and a single wooden chair.

"The light in here is dim, but low light is best." She maneuvered between the shelves and the table, inched her way through the furniture jam under the windows, and pulled the long floor-to-ceiling curtain shut, making the room more cave-like. "Natural light is hard on old documents." She shuffled over to the right-hand wall, moved the dust mop off to the side, and opened one of the deep drawers from one of the cabinets.

She took two pairs of white gloves from the drawer—like the ones Muggie wore in the museum—and handed one pair to me. "These go back in the drawer when you're done. Please don't touch anything without wearing them."

I slid them on. "Yes, ma'am."

She laid a flannel cloth the size of a place mat on the table. Then she read the labels on the other drawers, got to the one marked M through R, pulled it open, and gently lifted out a small, brown leather-bound book. "Okay. There you have it." She checked her watch. "I need to go. When you're done, put the diary back in the proper drawer, put the gloves away, and turn off the light."

"Do you want me to lock the door when I leave?"

"Nah. It's a super-old door and only locks with a key. I'll come back and lock up after my meeting."

I put my backpack on the table and sat, and then gently ran my hand over the cover. Even with the gloves on, the softness of the old leather was obvious. I eased the diary open. The pages were yellowed with age, and they crinkled when I touched them. Elizabeth's handwriting looked like something straight from the Declaration of Independence. I wondered how she kept her lines as straight as she did without using notebook paper.

Elizabeth began the journal right after they got to America. Some of the words were hard to decipher, but once I got used to her old-timey script, it got easier.

October 21, 1745

Papa gave me a new journal, stating I should write about the new world in a new book. Mama says it is an extravagant waste. But Papa says it is part of my schooling.

So I shall set out events faithfully—to please him.

We have been in the new land two months now—but this is the first chance I have had to write due to the fact we have been so busy. We have been building shelter—trying to get all the cabins up before the winter, though we hear winter is mild in this new land. Papa's been hunting and fishing, and I've been helping Mama with cleaning and drying the meat and fish. And between that and tending the families of the sick and dying we have had no time for much of anything else.

We have all been healthy, thank the good hand of Providence, but we have had to work hard so we could share with those women busy caring for their sick husbands or children. Yesterday I delivered dried venison and salted fish to the Reverend's widow and his poor son, Joseph. The whole township was in a pitiful state when he died. We loved him so.

But as much as everyone loved him, there was some dissention over his burial spot. Some said it was not fitting to bury the reverend where people would have to walk over him when they entered the house of worship. But his widow maintained it was no different than Westminster Abbey being the final resting place for so many. And in the end, she won the day. And he did love music so and he did bring the bell all the way over from England, so it does seem like a happy place for his bones to rest.

Several others have been buried as well. Isaac Cook, little Mary Shepherd died of the croupe, and Hildy Wheeler succumbed after a bite by a venomous snake. They are all buried in the graveyard out back of the church, of course. And several others have been sick. This heat here seems to suck the vigor out of a body. But thank the Good Lord no one else has died.

And thank Graciousness, too that the berry bushes have all been plentiful. And meat is finished drying. And the house is built and there is a warm fire in the hearth and now I can write. I shall write each month to record the bounty of the new world.

On any other day I would have found this fascinating. How differently they spoke. And lived! But I was in a hurry. As interesting as it was, none of this information would help me find the treasure. The date was too early. I needed entries from after her dad died. Anything written after 1748 might tell where she buried the treasure. I carefully flipped through the yellowed pages.

My eyes caught the word *death*. I stopped even though the year was wrong—1746.

Elizabeth's mom died giving birth. The baby died too. Maybe Elizabeth was too depressed to write after that because several months passed with no entries.

When the new entries started, a lot of them were about the war and her fears.

She was afraid for her father.

Afraid he would die.

Afraid she'd be an orphan.

Afraid she'd die.

And then in 1748 her fears came true.

January 26, 1748

I am at such loss. I can barely write these words. Father has died. I have no one left in Gifton. I am being sent to Virginia where I have distant family.

Yet a secret goes with me. Father's dying gift. I fear being found with it. Too much danger. For the time being it is safely hidden, and I'll return and claim it once I get settled in Virginia and find family I can trust.

My breath caught. Danger? What kind of treasure was dangerous? I read page after page, but nothing else even hinted at treasure.

The entries had long gaps.

She wrote about settling in Virginia.

She wrote about courting—which I guess was some old-fashioned way of saying dating—Nathaniel Pembroke.

She wrote about their wedding.

Zilch about the treasure…until almost eight years passed.

August 11, 1756

I have told Nathaniel there is great wealth in Gifton. He believes I am referring to the richness of the soil and available land. He is a knowledgeable farmer, and I am confident the ground will flourish under his care, and that Little Annabelle and I will be well provided for.

I never told him about the other treasure buried in the rich soil of Gifton. I'll never forget Papa's earnest expression on his deathbed. He was adamant that I not share the secret with suitors—he said it would attract cutthroats and cads. But, oh, how good it will be to tell Nathaniel.

Nay…I will not tell him. What if, in my absence, it has been discovered, or stolen? I do not want to give him false hope. I will show him instead. A joyous surprise indeed if it remains hidden and safe!

We have finalized all arrangements for our journey. I

know travel may be treacherous, especially on horseback and with a young babe, but I cannot help feeling great happiness at the thought of returning to Gifton.

Pretty soon after that, Elizabeth must've fallen from her horse and died, because it was the last entry. Plus, the photograph in the library had said Nathaniel moved to Gifton as a widower.

I ran my fingers gently over the pages. Is this how the rumors of buried treasure in Gifton got started? Elizabeth had died suddenly—thrown from her horse—taking the secret of the treasure with her to the grave. But Nathaniel must have found Elizabeth's diary after her death and read what she wrote. The story was then passed down to his kids.

A key scraped into the doorknob behind me. I just about jumped out of my chair from fright. Crud! I looked at my watch. I hadn't been in here that long. It couldn't be Miss Cornett. No way would she be done with her meeting. I didn't want her getting in trouble for letting me use the archives room alone. I needed to hide.

The doorknob rattled, and the key scraped again. I quickly, but gently, wrapped the flannel cloth around the diary and shoved it into my backpack.

I heard two kicks on the door as I darted behind the last sheet-covered shelf on the left.

The door swung open. I peeked around to see who it was. Muggie, wearing her emergency kit apron, came in, muttering about the door being unlocked. She bustled to the wooden bookcase near the windows, took an empty lamp and the large bottle of oil, and brought them to the table, where she filled the lamp, and lit it. She adjusted the wick up and down a few times, trying to get it to the perfect height so it would shed the maximum light without smoking.

Whew. She was just getting supplies for the museum. She'd leave and I'd go back to reading where I left off in the diary.

But she cracked open the door and leaned out. Then she shut the door again, locked it from the inside, and dropped the key back into her apron.

What was she doing?

CHAPTER 26

MUGGIE HURRIED TO THE covered junk pile at the back of the room.

I was crouched down as small as I could be, but if she looked to her left, she'd see me. Suddenly the dim light in the room felt way too bright. I didn't move. I didn't breathe.

She lifted the corner of the old sheet and pulled out—

What? I jerked in surprise when I saw her holding a heavy, antique frame, and I bumped the shelf behind me.

"Who's there?" Muggie barked, looking my way.

I slipped my backpack onto my shoulders, making ready to leave quickly, and nervously stepped out of the shadows. "It's just me, Muggie."

"Grady!" Her brow furrowed. "What are you doing here unsupervised?"

I fumbled for an excuse. "Oh, I…uh, umm… I was—" But my voice trailed off as I stared at the object in her hands.

Cherubs on an *empty* frame grinned back at me. What was it doing here? And where was my mom's Civil War sampler I'd put inside?

I scratched my forehead. "What are you doing with that?"

She looked down at what she held. "I found this broken in the dumpster a couple days ago. I fixed it and left it here to dry."

"But it's from the break-in at the Music Box. It's evidence," I said. "How did it get here? Don't the police need it?"

She drew the frame close. "No. Like I told you, I found this in the dumpster. It's for the museum." She set it on the table next to the lit lamp.

I shook my head. "That's the frame I sold to Arliss. Someone obviously removed the sampler and then tossed the frame."

She arched her brows at me for a moment. "Are you accusing *me*, the mayor's wife, of something nefarious?"

I swallowed. "No, no. Of—of course not," I stuttered. "But don't you think maybe, uh, we should give it to the police? It might have fingerprints on it."

She gave a high-pitched laugh. "Of course, it has fingerprints—mine! From when I retrieved it from the trash."

"I meant the thief's," I murmured.

She held up her hands. "Honey, the thief wore gloves."

Oh. Duh. That made sense.

But...Deputy Oringderff never mentioned anything about gloves, did she? Only that the thief wore men's boots, size 12.

"How do you know the thief wore gloves?" I asked.

She rolled her eyes with a theatrical sigh. "Winifred, who else?"

That also made sense.

Of course, Muggie wasn't the thief. But I knew that frame was the one I sold to Arliss. That frame was evidence and it needed to go to Deputy Oringderff. It was clear, though, that Muggie was not going to give it up. She was acting so weird. And she was glaring at me, like I was some kind of bug who'd invaded her picnic. Why was she so angry?

I shot a quick glance toward the door. I could have made a run for it—I was sure I could outrun her—but she had locked the door with the key. The key that was in her pocket.

"I'm sorry, Muggie." I hung my head, slumped toward the table. "You're probably right about the frame. It'll look nice in the museum." I plopped onto the chair. "I guess I'm not thinking straight. Dad and I are losing our home. If the sampler Eudora left us really had been a treasure map, it might have fixed everything." I left out a small laugh. "Whoever stole it is on a wild-goose chase."

Her glare softened. It was working. She'd be unlocking the door any minute.

"I better go home and help Dad pack. We've got to be out in two days."

I sensed her calculating gaze still on me, and I held my breath.

Her voice was calm when she answered. "I wasn't aware about your home—which means Winifred probably doesn't know either." She huffed. "No small feat keeping a secret from her. Kudos to your father." She tucked the frame back onto the pile and covered it back up with the sheet. Then she pulled out her key and headed for the door.

She was buying it. She was going to let me go. I sagged with relief.

I stood, adjusted my backpack, and pushed the chair in. "It was fun to imagine there was a treasure," I said. Thinking I'd just keep the nice, friendly conversation going. "I mean, it's not far-fetched to think someone might have hidden something, right?"

"Hmmphf." She stuck the key in the lock. "With all the chaos that came with war, I wouldn't be surprised. I suppose it makes sense that someone would hide treasure to keep it from the Yanks who were raiding every farm and plantation they passed."

Only the thief would know it was a Civil War sampler in that frame. "It was you," I blurted. The hairs on the back on my neck trembled. *Yanks…plantations.*

Only…I didn't *mean* to say it out loud. I slapped my hand over my mouth the minute the words came out.

Muggie spun around and locked eyes with mine. "What did you say?" she demanded.

My chest tightened.

I lowered my hand. "Nothing," I whispered. "I don't know anything."

"What exactly are you accusing me of?"

My pulse raced.

Think!

Think!

Think!

I couldn't yell for help. No one would hear. Maybe I could stall until Miss Cornett returned.

I took a deep breath. "I was just wondering how you knew it was a Civil War sampler."

She rolled her eyes. "I saw it in the diner along with the *entire town.*"

But she hadn't. I traded out Eudora's sampler for my mother's Civil War sampler, right before I'd taken it to the Music Box. I got to the store just as it closed. Arliss locked the door behind me when I left. The *only* people who saw the Civil War sampler were the McGinters. And the thief—the... the killer.

"Oh, that's right." I said, trying to sound innocent. "I forgot everyone had seen it at the diner."

She glared. Something in her eyes had changed. She stepped toward me. "Do you think I'm stupid?"

I darted backward, keeping the table between us, and kept talking. "You *killed* Arliss. How could you?"

"His death was an accident!"

My hands tightened to fists. "You could've just bought the sampler."

"I shouldn't have to buy what's already mine!" Her eyes grew wild. "I took care of Eudora and those cats—all those horrible cats. She had twenty litter boxes. Who do you think cleaned them every day? I did. I knew she had no relatives. She told me she'd leave me a treasure in her will. And then the old bat left the house to her cats! But when I saw she left the sampler for you, I knew that was the treasure she meant to leave *me*. It just must have slipped her mind, and she forgot to add me into the will. She was horrible at remembering things!"

I glanced to the door. *Where* was Miss Cornett?

Muggie kept talking. "Of course, I didn't want to frame Badger. But he made it so darn easy. The whole town knows he always keeps his boots on the front porch. Besides his defense attorney would certainly prove that whoever broke into the Music Box had stolen Badger's shoes and worn them to throw off the law."

"I–I–I won't tell anyone. I promise." Total lies, of course. The first thing I'd do is sprint to the police station. "Dad and I are leaving Gifton. I won't even live here anymore. Please let me go."

"Don't be foolish."

Maybe Muggie would let me out if I convinced her she had no choice but to turn herself in. I took a deep breath. "The police know everything."

"Impossible."

"Deputy Oringderff knows someone tried to break into our house. It—it was you. I saw your shadow before Ophelia chased you off. You broke a fingernail using the crowbar on our door. I gave it to Deputy Oringderff days ago," I lied. "Your fingerprints will be all over the crowbar. She has that too. She's processing it for prints."

She showed me her fingers. "I'm not missing a nail."

"You replaced it."

"Lots of people use these nails!" she retorted.

"But yours will have your DNA on it."

She slowly lowered her hands as her face turned white.

"Please. Unlock the door. Turn yourself in. You're not a horrible person. You just made a mistake. But—but you can fix it."

She paced back and forth in front of the table. "You don't understand what it's been like for me. You're just a kid, and you're poor! You've never had the finer things in life. I'm the mayor's wife! I should've been hosting parties and managing my husband's political career, but the fool lacks ambition. So instead, I'm stuck polishing and cleaning all those stupid artifacts and dealing with stupid tourists asking stupid questions all day long. The humiliation! I wanted what I was accustomed to—money, luxury, *real* jewelry." She touched her neck with her other hand. The pearls were gone, but a thin red graze marked her skin. "I'd almost made it out with the sampler when Arliss came downstairs. Made a grab for me but broke that worthless strand from my neck instead."

That explained why she'd been wearing a scarf the last few days. She'd been covering the mark left by the broken strand of pearls. The memory of sweeping up white beads at the Music Box after the break-in popped into my mind. I kicked myself for not recognizing at the time what they really were.

"Arliss wasn't supposed to die. He fell back into the shelf of instruments when he grabbed my necklace, and then all the shelves started falling. I just wanted the sampler." She glared at me. "I've spent hours studying that stupid embroidery. It makes no sense!"

I needed to give her a reason to let me out and she just gave it to me.

"You don't have the real sampler," I confessed. "I switched them."

She grabbed both sides of the table. "You're telling me

it's as *fake* as my pearls?" Her face turned the color of purple grapes.

I tried to hide my shaking. "I'll take you to the *real* sampler. I know where it is. You can still have the treasure."

"Sure—while you run and get the police. I don't think so."

"Please, just turn yourself in. I'm sure Deputy Oringderff will understand Arliss's death was an accident."

"Shut up! Just shut up. I need to think. I was so close." She flung out her arm and pointed. "This is all your fault!"

I was glad the table was between us, because she looked mad enough to murder me. "Miss Cornett knows I'm here. She'll be back any minute."

Muggie smirked. "Don't worry, I'll let her know you left." She backed slowly toward the door, never taking her eyes off me. "No one works in this wing of the building. No one would expect a child to be in the archives room unattended. I'll be long gone before anyone finds you locked in here."

I tried to dodge around the table so I could I lunge for the door.

But she dashed forward and shoved the table into me.

The oil lamp teetered.

I grabbed and steadied it before it could crash to the floor and explode in a ball of fire, but the refill bottle toppled over, and she hadn't put the cap on tightly. Oil poured to the floor.

That distraction was all Muggie needed to make her escape out the door. She sneered as she closed the door. The lock clicked into place, and the room went dark as she turned off the lights.

CHAPTER 27

THE FLICKERING FLAME FROM the oil lantern didn't give much light, but it was enough for me to see to get around the table. I made my way to the door and banged on it for ten minutes straight. No one came.

I turned to look at the windows on the back wall. Maybe they were big enough for me to slide through. If I could get them open. There was a wooden bookcase filled with museum stuff near the back wall, under the windows. I could use it as a ladder.

Even if the windows were painted shut, I could pound on them. Get someone's attention. Or maybe even break through by using something heavy. I could crawl through and escape to the outside. It'd be a short fall to the ground.

I headed toward the back wall. That's when my foot hit an

oil patch and skated out from under me. I jerked and clawed at the table for support, and in my flailing, I sideswiped the lamp. Glass shattered and oil splattered—all over the floor and the sheets that hung on the shelves.

Flames whooshed to life.

"Oh, crap!"

Tongues of fire licked the oil tracks, lapping them up.

I climbed onto the chair just as the oil-splattered sheets sprouted flames, which quickly climbed upward. The dusty books under the sheets ignited, spewing sparks in all directions.

Several of those sparks blew over to the pile of furniture that lay between me and the back wall. The baskets woven by some Indians long ago went up like matchsticks and then the antique chair caught. Flames were dancing all over the grandfather clock. It wouldn't be long before they grabbed hold and it turned into a towering inferno. An intense barrier of orange and yellow heat expanded between me and the back wall on that side of the room. Billowing smoke filled the air. Coughing, I scrambled from the chair, up on to the table, then jumped to the top of the waist-high wooden cabinets. On my hands and knees, I crawled beyond the fire.

Why hadn't the sprinkler system gone off yet?

I jumped down from the cabinets and yanked the floor-to-ceiling curtain from the window. The rod clattered to the floor.

I threw the curtain onto the blaze and stomped. But the flames flared out of both ends. I backed away.

Heat surrounded me. My eyes stung, and my lungs burned.

With both arms I swiped everything from the shelves of the wooden bookcase near the windows. Empty oil lamps, plates, figurines, and knickknacks crashed to the floor. Crunching over the debris, I shoved the bookcase toward the wall, tilting it so I could use it like a ladder.

My lungs screamed. I was running out of time.

I needed something to break the windows out. I spun around looking for something heavy. Anything. The curtain rod was too wimpy to break through the glass. Right next to me I saw the frame sticking out from under the sheet where Muggie had tucked it. That would work.

Clutching the frame with one arm, I climbed awkwardly up the bookshelf. Balancing on the top shelf, I struck the window. A grinning cherub broke off.

Flames licked at the base of the bookshelf.

I slammed the frame into the glass window again.

A tiny crack appeared.

And again.

The crack spider-webbed larger.

And again.

My lungs wanted to burst.

I swung one more time.

The window shattered, and thick smoke raced out around me. The flames behind me stretched higher, seeking air. I knocked away as much glass as I could. I dragged myself over the sill and gripped the edge. My eyes burned from the smoke, and everything was blurry. I didn't know for sure how far the drop was. I closed my eyes and let go.

I fell to the grass and then rolled on my back, sucking in air, trying to clear my lungs. I looked back to the library. I'd only jumped about ten feet. Maybe a little more. I didn't care.

Mr. Russ, on the opposite side of the street, was sweeping the sidewalk in front of his insurance shop. He stopped, gaped at the smoke rising from the window, threw down his broom, and ran toward me. "Fire!" he yelled. "Fire at the library!"

More voices hollered. They came closer. I slid my backpack off, rolled over, and stared at the sky, still gulping in fresh air. Ophelia's furry face appeared over mine. She licked me between barks and howls, cleaning the soot off my face. It was not a good feeling—dog drool smearing smoky soot around. But I was too weak to push her away. Besides, she was trying to help. I loved that dog.

After a few minutes, she felt she had finished bathing me, I guess, because she disappeared.

Mr. Russ knelt and touched my shoulder. "You all right?"

I closed my eyes, trying to concentrate on breathing in fresh air. And trying to take stock of how I was feeling. I tried to answer, but the words came out as a raspy croak. I nodded to assure Mr. Russ I was okay.

Ophelia returned and dropped something on me.

"You got a squirrel on your chest, son," Mr. Russ said. "Don't worry, it's not dead. Just a tad confused and a little wet from dog slobber." He nudged it away with his broom.

From the firehouse on the end of Main Street, two blocks over, the siren wailed.

The firetruck came.

Then Deputy Oringderff. She took one look at me and got on her radio, calling for an ambulance to be sent out from Anaston.

~~~~~

About a half hour later, the fire was out, and Ida Rose was feeding oatmeal cookies to the growing crowd of onlookers that huddled near the open back door of the ambulance. Clemmie and Thad sat inside with me as a paramedic wrapped gauze around my left arm where glass from the window had cut me. Thad found the box of rubber gloves and started blowing air into a glove like a balloon. Miss Cornett stood just outside the ambulance, hands wringing and chin quivering. Thad eyed her nervously.

My backpack rested between my ankles on the stretcher. It was pretty torn up—and that was too bad, since Dad didn't have money to buy me a new one.

"Better that than your back being shredded," Clemmie said when she saw me looking at it.

"It's no big deal," I croaked. "But all those old books..."

Too bad they all burned. They were in that room to be kept safe. I looked again at my backpack, wondering if Elizabeth Pembroke's journal was shredded or if it had survived.

The rubber-glove balloon was almost the size of Thad's head.

"Don't you worry about the books, sugar," Miss Cornett said. "As long as you're okay, that's all that matters." And then she burst into tears.

Pfft! The rubber glove shot out of the ambulance and landed on Miss Cornett's shoulder. Thad stared wide-eyed. "I panicked. Sorry."

Deputy Oringderff handed the glove to Miss Cornett as she climbed into the ambulance. Thad and Clemmie silently scooted over to make room on the narrow bench, but didn't offer to leave, and she didn't ask them to. She sat next to Thad.

"You okay, Grady?" she asked.

I nodded and kept the oxygen mask on.

She glanced at the paramedic, who gave her a thumbs-up.

Only then did she pull her notebook from her pocket. "Feel like answering some questions?"

I eyed the mayor who stood in the crowd at the back of the ambulance. I didn't want to say anything in front of everyone, but the longer I waited, the more time Muggie had to escape. I lowered the oxygen mask. "Muggie killed Arliss," I rasped.

Gasps rippled from the nearest onlookers. Whispers traveled to those farther back. And Mayor Shore went whiter than the chef's hat he wore at Gifton's annual bake-off competition.

Deputy Oringderff gestured to an officer who herded everyone away from the ambulance. A frown creased her brow. "Explain."

The paramedic handed me a bottle of water. I drank half. The water felt cool and helped soothe my throat. Then I told Deputy Oringderff how Muggie confessed to breaking into the Music Box, stealing the sampler, and killing Arliss. And then how she locked me in the room. I finished the water in between giving details. The paramedic handed me another one. Deputy Oringderff took notes. She listened and wrote, only stopping me when she had a question. Then she got out but stayed near the doors.

Evrol screeched into the town square. Dad parked—if you can call driving up onto the courthouse grass parking— and sprinted toward me. Clemmie dragged Thad out of the ambulance as he argued with her.

"Grady!" Dad climbed into the ambulance and pulled me hard against him. He squeezed me so tight I could breathe better when I was in the fire, but I didn't mind. He hadn't hugged me that tight since Mama died. He relaxed after a minute and released me.

The fire chief came over. "We saved the library, but the archives room and the one next to it are a total loss." He looked past Deputy Oringderff to me. "You're one lucky young man. That was smart using the bookcase as a ladder."

Dad paled. "What happened?"

The fire chief thumbed behind him to the firemen putting away their hoses. "The place reeks of arson. There was an accelerant."

Dad spun, his fists tightened and loosened. "Are you accusing my son of starting that fire?"

"Don't worry, Kevin." Deputy Oringderff put her hand on his arm. "That's not what happened. I'll fill you in. Just give me a minute." She told the dispatcher to put out a BOLO for Muggie from the radio mic on her shoulder.

"What's a BOLO?" I asked.

She said, "It stands for 'Be on the Lookout.' We'll find her."

"Why are you looking for Muggie?" Dad asked.

"She killed Arliss," I croaked.

"Apparently, Muggie stole the cross-stitch sampler you

inherited from Eudora Klinch," Deputy Oringderff said. "She thought it would lead her to a treasure. She tried to break into your house to steal it first. Then the next night she broke into the Music Box."

"Wow," Dad said. "Who would have suspected Muggie?"

"Well, it gets worse. When Grady saw her with the frame, she locked him in a room at the library."

Dad was appalled. "She locked him in and set the place on fire?"

"She wasn't trying to kill him, any more than she was trying to kill Arliss. She just wanted to keep him locked up so he couldn't tell anyone while she made her escape. But when the fire started, he couldn't get out. We very nearly had a second death on our hands. Thankfully, you've got one smart kid here." She winked at me. "Grady, where's the press-on nail?"

"My bedroom."

She looked at Dad. "I need to send a crime scene unit to your house right away to photograph and dust for prints on your front door. I know it's been a few days since the break-in, but we might get lucky. They'll also need to collect the crowbar and nail. Since Muggie never made it inside, it shouldn't take too long, but they need to collect that evidence."

Dad nodded. "As soon as we get the all clear from the paramedic, we'll meet them there."

The deputy joined the fire chief, who stood with the mayor, who looked lost. His face was drawn. No hat perched on his head. He got a story all right, but not the one he wanted.

I faced the paramedic. "Can I go now?"

"Drink lots of water." She shot Dad a glance. "And no strenuous activity for the next few days."

With my parched, scratchy throat, I didn't need any reminders to drink water.

I climbed down from the ambulance. Dad draped his arm over my shoulder, and I leaned in to him as we walked to Evrol. I climbed in, rested against the seat, and hugged my backpack. Curious about the diary, I peeked into my bag and saw that the book was still wrapped in the cloth—still intact and clean.

I didn't touch it. I was a mess. I flipped the truck mirror down. Black streaks of ash, soot, and grime covered my face and arms. I reeked of oil, smoke, and sweat. My clothes were destined for the trash—one less thing I'd have to pack for our move.

Even though my throat hurt, I spilled everything to Dad on the way home. I mean *everything*. From switching the samplers, to learning about the symbols and dates, to Elizabeth Radcliffe becoming Elizabeth Pembroke. I told him I had Elizabeth Pembroke's journal in my backpack and what I'd learned about her and her family and the War of Jenkins's Ear.

When I told him about Pastor Jeremy finding us digging in the cemetery, he chuckled.

I told him how frustrated I was with the clue of three layers of stone and wood.

And about how smart Eudora Klinch really was.

"Must be genetic," he said when I mentioned that last part. "Your mother was really smart. She was a genius at puzzles. And she would have loved a good treasure hunt. And you obviously take after your mama." He quietly added, "You are like her in so many ways."

"I'm sorry I kept the sampler. I just wanted to find the treasure so bad. I knew she'd understand."

"And you didn't think I would?"

I nodded.

"That's my fault." He kept his eyes on the road. "I'm sorry."

We turned onto our dirt road, Evrol surrounded by puffs of clay dust. "Every time I see you, I see her. Did you know that, Grady?"

"No."

"Well, it's true." He parked beside the police van and turned Evrol's engine off. He rested his head against the back window. We had to wait for the cops to finish with the crime scene and let us into the house.

"I'm like you too," I said. "I just didn't realize it before."

He cast a glance toward me. "Oh?"

"I'm determined."

He chuckled and ruffled my hair. "Your mama used to say stubborn, but I like 'determined' better." Then he looked at my backpack. "You'll need to return that journal to the library, but maybe use the book drop instead of going inside this time?"

I rolled my eyes at his sorry humor, but really it felt good to joke with him. We hadn't done that in forever.

We would have no treasure.

We would have no home.

We would have to move.

But we would have each other, and somehow, I was okay with that.

CHAPTER 28

DAD LET ME SLEEP in the next morning, but Thad and Clemmie were less generous. They tapped at my window, so I crawled out of bed with scratchy throat and aching chest.

"What are you doing here?" I asked.

Thad climbed in first. "To help you pack."

Clemmie followed. "Your room is such a mess. If Muggie had torched this instead, I think it'd be cleaner."

She was right. Papers, clothes, books, and a bunch of other junk covered my floor. I laughed but turned and blinked several times to keep tears from forming. I'd miss Clemmie's humor. I'd miss a lot of things about her. Thad too.

"Let me get dressed and I'll get some boxes." I picked up a shirt and a pair of shorts from the floor and changed in the bathroom.

Dad kept the boxes in the living room. I dashed down the

hall and brought a couple to Clemmie and Thad. "I'll be back with more in a minute." I had two in my hands as Dad came in the front door.

"Morning. Was that Thad and Clemmie I saw climbing in your window?"

"Yup."

"They do know we have a front door, right?"

I shrugged. "No point in starting to use it now."

He eyed the boxes. "You working on your room?"

"They're going to help."

"That'd be great. I'm almost done with the workshop." He took a deep breath, and his shoulders fell. He hadn't shaved lately and had bags under his eyes. I hadn't noticed them before.

"You look tired," I said.

"I made coffee this morning but forgot I packed the mugs." He shrugged. "Not smart."

I thought for a moment. "I got one in my room."

I rushed to get the mug off my desk. Clemmie and Thad glanced up.

"I'll be right back."

Back in the kitchen, I dumped the pencil shavings and dust into the trash and rinsed the mug out before handing it to Dad.

"Number One Mom," he said. "What happened to the handle?"

"It broke. I tried to fix it, but it never stuck. I probably didn't hold the handle to the glue long enough. Couldn't fix that hairline crack either, but at least coffee doesn't leak out of it."

"Broken things take a while to set right, and even then there can still be problems." He looked at me and then he laughed. "Just like Evrol. I'm not sure how many more times I'm going to be able to fix him."

I watched him pour coffee into the cup and take a sip. Sometimes broken things couldn't be fixed to be exactly like they were before. But that didn't mean they wouldn't work out okay in the end anyway.

I went back to join Clemmie and Thad in my room. The box I'd started packing Friday night wasn't full yet, so I reached for the pile of clothes on my desk. Eudora's Gershwin piano book fell off the desk and landed, splayed open, on the floor. As I picked it up, a bit of writing on the sheet music caught my eye.

Different methods of touching the keys will result in different representation of timbre.

Timbre? Why would lumber be mentioned in a music book...unless timbre wasn't actually talking about wood. I dropped the book onto the bed, knelt by Clemmie, and started pulling out books she was neatly loading into a box.

"What are you doing?" she asked. "I don't think you understand how packing is supposed to work."

"I need my dictionary."

I finally found it and flipped it open. I thumbed through the Ts, searching for *timbre*.

Timber right.

Timber wolf.

Timberwork.

Timbre: Noun. The characteristic quality of sound produced by a particular instrument or voice.

The riddle ran through my head.

Seeke ye first the Kingdome of God.
Stay close to all ye held dear. Matthew 17:39
Three layers of stone and one of timbre.

The wheels in my head turned and whirled. Thoughts and ideas jumped around. Something perched on the tip of my brain, but I couldn't quite catch it.

But then... It was like a bell rang.

"Oh man," I muttered.

"What?" asked Thad.

Clemmie stared at me.

I set the dictionary down. "I know where the treasure is."

Thad raised a brow. "We've heard that before."

I waved his comment away. "Yeah, yeah, I know. But this time I'm sure. Clemmie, get your phone and look at the photo of the sampler."

She scrolled to the image.

"I was right when I said the 'Seeke ye first the Kingdome of God' part meant the church."

"Nope. Can't be," Thad argued. "We already know there aren't enough layers of stone at the church."

"Before Muggie tried to torch me, I read some of Elizabeth's diary. I found the third layer yesterday—only I didn't make the connection until just *now*."

I got my backpack and pulled out the gloves and Elizabeth's diary.

Thad's eyes widened. "You stole her diary?"

"I prefer to think I saved it from the fire. Don't worry, I'll return it to Miss Cornett."

I slipped the gloves on and gently opened to the page I wanted. "Listen to this." I read the part about the bell tower being built over the grave of the reverend as a special way to remember him.

Yesterday I delivered dried venison and salted fish to the Reverend's widow and his poor son, Joseph. The whole township was in a pitiful state when he died. We loved him so.

But as much as everyone loved him, there was some dissention over his burial spot. Some said it was not fitting to bury the reverend where people would have to walk over him when they entered the house of worship. But his widow maintained it was no different than burying folks in Westminster Abbey. And in the end, she won the day. And he did love music so and he did bring the bell all the way over from England, so it does seem like a happy place for his bones to rest.

"I don't see the connection," Clemmie said.

I held up a finger, telling her to wait. "Who was Gifton's first preacher?"

"Joseph Stone," Clemmie said. She paused, then added. "I thought." She narrowed her eyes, thinking. "Winifred always says her family tree is full of preachers. And she can map her ancestors all the way back to the Reverend Joseph Stone. But from that diary it sounds like there was another reverend before Joseph."

I nodded. "Joseph Stone had a father." I leaned in. "The

third layer of stone…is Joseph Stone's dad—the Reverend *Stone*. No one ever talks about him because there is no marker in the cemetery for him."

Another architect's name, Frank Gehry, slipped from Thad's lips.

Clemmie paced. "You're telling me a dead body is the third layer. That's totally creepy."

"The church bell tower would've already been built when Elizabeth needed to bury the treasure, so I think she buried it near the *base* of the bell tower not actually under his body."

She stopped pacing. "What about the timber part of the riddle?"

I picked up the dictionary. "'Timbre' isn't the English spelling of 'timber' like we'd been thinking. It's not even pronounced the same. It's pronounced *tam-ber*. It's a musical term and points back to the bell tower. Same when she uses the word 'hear.' It's a homophone. Everything points to the bell tower, which is part of the church. The treasure's been on our property this whole time! Remember what Pastor Jeremy said? The Knee Scraper is the old church foundation. It all fits. What do you think?" My excitement grew.

They looked at each other and then to me.

Clemmie grinned. "Elizabeth was brilliant. I would've loved to be on a debate team with her. Grady, I think you're brilliant too."

"Everything *seems* to fit," Thad said, "but we've been wrong before."

I stood. "There's only one way to find out."

CHAPTER 29

WE SPRINTED OUT THE front door.

"Dad!" I called.

He peered around the workshop door, holding an electric sander. "What's wrong?"

I ran to him. "I know where the treasure is. Can we look—all of us? You too."

He turned back into the workshop.

I exchanged nervous glances with Clemmie and Thad. "Stay here."

I stepped into the workshop. It was dim and smelled of sawdust. It smelled like Dad. I'd miss it. But if we found the treasure, maybe we could stay. "Dad. It's an adventure—" I swallowed. "One last time, and then I'll let it go. I promise. Please."

He placed the sander in the box and then turned. "I'll get the shovels."

~~~~

We made the ten-minute walk to the Knee Scraper in seven.

"Okay, Mr. Architect, where do you think the bell tower stood?" I asked Thad.

He handed Clemmie his shovel and walked around the stone surface, pausing to study the overgrown floor, pulling back plants and small tree limbs when necessary, his face screwed in concentration.

After several minutes he straightened. "Here, I think." He stopped on the side opposite to where Dad, Clemmie, and I stood. "See how the foundation is smaller here, but bigger there? Kinda like a front porch…" He pointed farther back. "And all that was the church proper."

We hurried over to the front-porch section. "The diary said that people had to walk over him to enter the worship service." It was about eight feet on all three of its sides, although the saplings and overgrowth made it hard to be sure.

I stepped off onto the forest floor. "The ground feels softer here than at the monument outside of town." I tapped my shovel on the dirt and leaves.

Dad looked upward. "The shade canopy helps keep the ground from being sunbaked."

"Then it should be easier to dig." Clemmie stepped down and faced me. "This is your treasure hunt. You're in charge. What's the plan?"

Thad whistled. "Never thought I'd ever hear Clementine Powell say someone *else* was in charge."

She grinned.

I swallowed. "Dad, how about you and I dig near here." I pointed.

"No strenuous activity, remember? I'll dig, you supervise."

I was going to argue, but my chest was hurting, truth be told. "Thad and Clemmie—y'all take that area there. I don't know how deep we need to go or if we're looking for a trunk, a chest, a box, or something else. Elizabeth wrote that the treasure was dangerous, so be careful."

Dad said, "If Elizabeth's dad brought it back from a raid like you think, my guess is it would fit in his knapsack or satchel."

"Good point." Thad nodded.

Clemmie pushed her shovel into the ground. "Maybe it's a solid-gold dagger."

"One more thing," I said. "We should probably dig a trench instead of individual holes. That way we won't miss anything."

Dad placed a hand on my shoulder. "Even if we don't find the treasure, Grady, I'm proud of you."

I smiled and breathed in the scent of freshly turned dirt that filled the air as they dug. This time, it smelled more like a new start than a bad memory.

Every time a shovel thudded against a tree root, or tinked from nicking stone, my heart threatened to burst with excitement, only to drop with disappointment a moment later.

Thad hit another root and groaned. "If I hear one more *thunk*, I'm going to lose it." He plopped down on the foundation and laid his shovel beside him. "You brought water, right, Grady?"

Dad had filled a thermos and put cups in my bag. "I need water too. Anyone else?"

Clemmie raised her hand.

Dad shook his head and jammed his shovel into his hole. A *shunk* sounded.

Everyone stopped and stared.

Thad stood. "That sounded different."

Dad yanked the shovel from the two-foot-deep hole, and I dropped to my knees. Lying on my stomach, I carefully scooped handfuls of dirt to the side. Dad lay next to me and helped.

My fingers brushed against something firm and angular, like maybe the corner of a trunk. "I feel it!" I grinned at Dad. "It's here! Right here! Help me clear this away."

We brushed away a final thin layer of dirt.

"It looks like a wooden box. Most of it is still buried." I stood and got a shovel. "We need to dig around it."

Thad climbed onto the foundation. "It's not a coffin, is it?"

I didn't know how big the wooden box was, but I could tell it was too small to be Reverend Stone's coffin. Thad must've realized the same thing, because he heaved a giant sigh after taking a peek.

"Let's go easy," Dad said. "We don't want to damage what's there."

I wanted to dig with a fury, but Dad was right. Who knew how fragile the box was or what condition it was in?

I handed him the shovel. "You're the one who works with wood. You dig it out."

Dad dug carefully around the box. It felt like it took him forever, but probably only a few minutes passed before he stepped away and pushed his shovel into the pile of dirt he'd created. "Your turn now."

I knelt. The trunk was small—about the size of two shoeboxes side by side—and its hinges were all rusty and crusty.

Clemmie clapped. "It's an actual treasure chest! Hurry! Pull it out!"

"Is it heavy?" Dad asked. "Do you need help?"

"I'm just trying to be careful." The wood looked like it could crumble if I touched it. I lifted it gently and set it on the ground next to them.

My dry throat ached, and my heart crashed against my ribs.

I brushed the last dirt clods off the box. There was a small lock on the clasp. I tugged at it.

"It's locked," I said.

Dad handed me a shovel. "Try gently knocking the hinges with the tip," Dad suggested. "The wood might be decayed enough you can coax them off."

I nodded. "Good idea."

After a few short nudges from the shovel, the hinges were freed. I lifted the lid.

A bundle of old fabric rested inside.

"Michael Graves," Thad uttered.

Dad leaned in for a closer look. "That looks like oilcloth, or rather, what's left of oilcloth."

I lifted the bundle from the box to unwrap it. It was heavy, but not as heavy as I'd expect a bar of gold to be. Shucks.

Under the dingy gray cloth was some kind of animal hide. "It's in better shape than the oilcloth."

Dad touched it. "Leather."

Clemmie bounced on her toes. "What's inside?"

I unwrapped the folds of the leather.

A face stared back at me.

Thad apparently ran out of architect's names and switched to building styles. "Holy Greek Revival. That's creepy. Is that a voodoo doll? Was there voodoo in Georgia back then?"

Clemmie flicked him on the head. "It's a rag doll, dork brain, not a voodoo doll."

A doll? I kicked the ground. "What the heck! What's with people thinking arts and crafts are treasure? First the sampler, now a doll, what's next?"

I handed it to Dad.

"Pretty heavy for a rag doll." He squeezed it. "Something doesn't feel right." He unwound strips of fabric that made up the clothing and pulled the head off the doll's body.

"A cross!" I said. A big one. About as long as one of my shoes. It looked like solid gold, with dark-green gemstones bordering the edge.

Dad handed it to me. "Definitely looks like something you'd see in a Catholic church. So your guess that Elizabeth's dad took Spanish treasure on a raid is a good one, Grady."

The weight felt beautiful. Heavy and cool. All my earlier disappointment vanished. We'd finally found it.

"Are these emeralds?" I asked, running my fingers over the stones.

"I think so," Dad said. "This was back before people made fake glass gemstones, I'm pretty sure." He winked at me. "Maybe this used to be attached to a staff or stood on an altar. Something used during mass, perhaps?"

"So that's why Elizabeth wrote that the treasure was

dangerous," I said. "There was religious freedom in Georgia— except for Catholics. They weren't allowed because Spain was Catholic. If Elizabeth was found with this, the colony governors might think she sympathized with the Spanish—a traitor. That definitely would've been dangerous."

Clemmie nodded. "Disguising the cross as a rag doll and hiding it until she could figure out what do was smart."

"The question is, what do *we* do now?" I asked. "Do we cash it in? Clemmie and Thad deserve a cut, Dad. They've been in on the treasure hunt with me all along."

Dad hunched his shoulders. "I don't know if we're allowed to keep it. We need to ask someone who knows the law."

"Mr. Burns?" I asked.

Thad pulled out his phone and handed it to Dad. "Call him now. See what he says."

Dad gently wrapped up the gold cross and laid it in the box. "I don't have his number with me. It's back at the house."

CHAPTER 30

THAD, CLEMMIE, AND I sat on the sofa while Dad and Mr. Burns spoke forever on the phone in his room. My leg bounced up and down. Clemmie finally pressed her hand down on my leg. "You're going to break through the floor at the rate you're going."

I looked at the closed door. "What's taking so long?"

Dad eventually came out. He was not looking like he'd just won the lottery.

"Well?" I swallowed.

"You're not going to like it." Dad plopped into Mama's rocking chair. "Mr. Burns says we can't keep it."

"What?" I squealed. "Why not?"

"This isn't a case of finders keepers. The cross wasn't lost by someone, and we just happened to find it. It was *stolen* from the

Spanish government." He ran his hands back and forth along the chair's arms.

"Maybe Mr. Burns is wrong. We can—"

"He's not." Dad cut me off before I could suggest we get a second opinion. "This is not the first bit of Spanish treasure found in these parts. There have been several cases. He told me about them. Spain has historical records—ships' manifests—and they can prove ownership of all these items that were stolen. I'm sorry, Grady."

"So basically, if you kept it, you'd cause an international incident," Clemmie said. "That sucks."

Dad sighed. "I agree. Mr. Burns is on his way over. He's going to do what he can to help us. Maybe there's a reward."

"It won't be as much as the treasure's worth though," Clemmie grumbled.

"We don't need it to be worth that much," I said. "Just enough to pay the bills and make ends meet."

Dad nodded. "Even if there is no reward, it'll be okay, Grady. The camper will be cool in the summer and warm in the winter. And we'll get back on our feet again."

Thad pulled out his phone. "If they're going to take the cross and put it in a museum, I say we get a group photo so we'll at least always have that."

Clemmie told us where to stand and Thad didn't argue.

About an hour later Mr. Burns arrived, along with Deputy Oringderff, who would give him a police escort to the Spanish consulate in Atlanta.

"I appreciate your willingness to come, Deputy Oringderff," Mr. Burns said.

"I was headed to Atlanta anyway." She turned to me. "It's good news for all y'all, but I'm sure you'll sleep better at night, Grady, knowing Muggie Shore was arrested about thirty minutes ago at the airport trying to arrange travel to the Marshall Islands. It appears she was following in her uncle's footsteps and hoping to avoid extradition. I'm bringing her back to stand trial in Tipton County."

Thad and Clemmie high-fived. Relief swelled inside me. I didn't *think* I was in danger, but knowing she'd been caught made me feel loads better.

"May I see this piece that's caused such chaos, please?" Mr. Burns asked.

"Sure." I led him and Deputy Oringderff over to the kitchen table. They admired the treasure while I explained how we put the clues from the sampler together and solved the riddle.

"What a find," Deputy Oringderff said. "Definitely has historical value. I'll reach out to the archaeological department at Georgia Eastern University. Maybe they can send a team out to look for the first Reverend Stone's remains. He should be laid to rest in the cemetery." She let out a small laugh. "Winifred should be glad of another ancestor to recite from."

I rewrapped the cross, placed it in the chest, and silently said goodbye to my dream of a new house with central air.

Thad, Clemmie, and I headed for my room, leaving Deputy Oringderff, Dad, and Mr. Burns talking about whether it was legal to remove human remains from a grave.

"I don't know if this was the best day of my life or the worst." I dropped onto my bed. "I can't tell."

When Mama was still alive, we'd gone to the beach for vacation one summer. I had watched shells ride the waves to the shore, only to be dragged back by the tide. That was sort of how I felt. My chance to stay in Gifton had been swept away.

But that wave…finding that cross—It was the biggest thrill of my life so far.

I nudged an empty box with my toe. "I don't know what to do. Do I keep packing? Or will there be a reward big enough for us to stay?"

"Good question," Clemmie said. "Maybe a compromise? Clean this mess up, get organized, and then if you need to pack, you get it done fast."

"And throw the trash out," Thad said. "You need to do that even if you end up staying." He scooped up a handful of mail from the floor.

I smacked my forehead with my palm. "Eudora's mail! Quick, give it to me. I gotta give it to Mr. Burns before he leaves."

~~~~~

The next day after lunch, Dad and I drove to the bank so he could sign paperwork, officially giving up our home. Miss Kline, the bank manager, led us to a small conference room.

She poured Dad a glass of water. "I'm sorry, Kevin. I truly wish there was something I could do."

She laid papers in front of Dad. "Look through those if you want. Most are missed payment statements and notices. The board of directors insisted I give them to you." She apologized again. "Please sign the last two pages."

Dad picked up the pen.

"Wait!" The double doors flew open. Mr. Burns nearly tripped over the slightly raised threshold. "Don't sign anything!"

Miss Kline startled in her chair. "Gracious! Who are you?"

"Myron Burns of Burns, Burns, and Burns."

She relaxed. "Oh yes, the boy band."

He dropped his briefcase on the conference table and tried to catch his breath. "I am *not* in a band. I'm an attorney." He took out a handkerchief and mopped his forehead.

Her eyes widened. "I can assure you everything is on the up-and-up, Mr. Burns." She turned to Dad. "You didn't need to go through the expense of hiring a lawyer. I wouldn't try to cheat you."

Mr. Burns collapsed into a chair and held up a finger. "One moment, please."

Miss Kline hurried to pour Mr. Burns a glass of water. She looked both concerned and confused.

Mr. Burns gulped half the water and took one more deep breath.

Dad reached for his own glass.

Mr. Burns straightened in his chair and smoothed his jacket and tie, reestablishing his dignity after his frenzied entrance. "That boy—the one with the weird name who likes squirrels—uh, Ophelia is it?"

Dad choked on his water. "Thaddeus."

Mr. Burns nodded. "Yes, him. He told me you were here. A very important piece of information has come into my hands." He leaned closer and held Dad's gaze. "A *very* important piece of information."

My heart thundered. *I* leaned forward. "Is it about the treasure?"

"No. Something different."

"Does it impact today's proceedings?" Miss Kline asked.

"Indeed, it does." He clicked open his briefcase, pulled out a file folder, and laid it in front of him. "It has to do with Mr. Nathaniel Pembroke, who you may or may not know, was a highly influential member of the Gifton settlement when our country was first forming."

Dad shot me a quick glance. "We're familiar with his story."

Mr. Burns kept talking. "I won't spend too much time on the family but humor me for a moment. Nathaniel had a daughter, Annabelle. She married Charles Dore and they had a son, Ethan. Charles was killed during the American Revolution. When Annabelle died a few years later, Nathaniel Pembroke *adopted* Ethan, his grandson. So, Ethan's name changed from Dore to Pembroke."

"He took the family name *and* also took over the family business after his grandfather's death in 1799. Ethan married and had several daughters, and one son. Daniel Pembroke."

Mr. Burns took a breather and reviewed his notes. "The Pembroke family grew wealthy through tobacco farming, but their fortune—most of it, anyway—went up in smoke during the Civil War. Literally. Their fields were burned."

"Yeah," I said, "almost the whole town burned."

Mr. Burns nodded. "After the property loss and destruction of the Civil War, many people left and started fresh somewhere else, yet Daniel saw the potential in rebuilding Gifton. But people needed work and a way to support their families." He flipped open the file folder, removed a copy of an old newspaper article, and slid it across the table to Dad and me.

"According to the *Tipton County Herald,* in June 1865, Daniel used what was left of his family's fortune to buy the land the town square currently sits on, plus a couple other parcels."

Mr. Burns leaned back and folded his hands. "The article explains that his family had loved Gifton and had supported it through the Revolutionary War. He wanted to carry on that legacy, so he rebuilt many of the businesses and signed lease-purchase agreements with the merchants. They had a livelihood and would own their own businesses, but in the meanwhile, he was their landlord."

"Not a bad plan." Miss Kline nodded.

Mr. Burns pulled some papers from the folder. "Wanting to ensure financial security for his family and their descendants, Daniel didn't allow lease-purchase agreements for any stores on the east side of the square. His family would always have property holdings there."

"Pembroke Avenue," I whispered.

"Yes." He patted the papers. "These are copies of the deeds. Every storefront on Pembroke Avenue is still Pembroke property."

Dad asked, "But how does that—"

"Eudora Klinch's great-great-great-grandfather was Daniel Pemboke. And you, Grady, as you know, are her next of kin." He pushed his glasses farther up on his nose and glanced between Miss Kline and Dad.

Dad looked from me to Mr. Burns. "Are you saying what I think you're saying?"

"What I am saying, Mr. Judd, is not only do you already *own* the land you're living on—that was one of the parcels he bought—but you also own all the property along Pembroke Avenue"—he looked at Miss Kline—"including this bank."

When Miss Kline left us so we could ask Mr. Burns the thousands of questions we had, she had tears in her eyes. I think they were the happy kind adults sometimes cry. She and Mama had been good friends, and it killed her that the bank's board of directors forced the foreclosure. She gave Dad and me hugs.

Mr. Burns turned to me. "We'd still be sorting through her accounts if you hadn't found and handed over that mail yesterday. In a bag of cat food, of all places. One letter was a monthly statement from Rauls Property Management."

"But why wasn't this in her will?" Dad asked.

Mr. Burns clicked his briefcase shut. "I suspect Eudora forgot she had this property. She had income as a museum curator, and she had Social Security. She didn't ever need the money from the Pembroke holdings. She got monthly statements but never accessed the account, and when her mind went, I doubt she knew what the statements were. She was unmarried and had no children, so no one knew to look for this account. Our offices didn't draw up her will or we would have known about this. She did her will on one of those internet sites. We were assigned as executors of her estate because she didn't name one." He frowned, putting a crease in his unibrow. "These do-it-yourself legal forms on the internet cause more mischief."

"What if I threw that mail away?" I asked.

"Oh, we would have found this eventually. Next month a statement would have been sent to the cats, I suppose."

Those cats! I was afraid to ask, but it would be better to know the truth than to have another treasure taken away. "Why don't the cats inherit this property?" I asked. "Why does it go to us?"

Mr. Burns stood and picked up his briefcase. "The will was very clear. The cats got the house and all its contents, and they also got the savings account in the local bank to support them for years to come. The rest of the estate went to next of kin."

Dad stood and shook Mr. Burns's hand. "And you say that Eudora never accessed her account?"

"Not a penny."

"How much is in there exactly?"

"Let's just say you'll be rich enough to buy a new boat when your other one gets wet."

"We don't own a boat," Dad whispered.

Mr. Burns winked. "Go get yourselves one."

CHAPTER 31

THANKS TO WINIFRED, NEARLY all of Gifton—minus the mayor and Muggie—showed up at the church for a spontaneous party Pastor Jeremy threw for us. His skills with hot dogs on a grill even coaxed Ophelia away from chasing squirrels. He and Dad spent a good chunk of the evening talking, and at some point, I heard Dad say he'd see him Sunday.

Charlie wandered around the fellowship hall refilling everyone's sweet tea, and Badger kept cracking jokes about being sprung from the pokey.

Miss Arlene and Winifred sat at the same table, heads together gossiping, but as some point Miss Arlene excused herself and shuffled over to where Clemmie, Thad, and I sat eating.

She lowered herself into the chair next to me with a sigh.

"I bet this was a water hydrant kind of day for you, wasn't it, Grady?" She reached over and squeezed my hand.

"Yes, ma'am. A total drencher."

She patted my hand. "It's probably for the best really. If life always went as we expected it to, we'd never know how much capacity we have for resilience, grace, and a whole bunch of other qualities."

"And we'd never be surprised," Clemmie said. "Just like I'm not surprised by the fact Thad is trying to stuff that whole brownie into his mouth right now."

Miss Arlene chuckled. "I do love a good surprise. I meant to tell y'all that I researched some of those antiques we brought back from Eudora's house. When they sell—and I have buyers for a couple already—the money they'll bring in will help put things right with the Music Box."

"That's great," Clemmie and I said together.

Thad nodded and mumbled with a mouthful of brownie.

Even though the night was warm and the mosquitoes were out, Thad, Clemmie, and I sat outside on Evrol's tailgate, kicking our legs back and forth enjoying the time alone. Normally I'd have been worried the tailgate might fall off with all that movement, but tonight wasn't one for worries.

Clemmie nudged me with her shoulder. The smell of her

coconut lotion hung in the air. "According to Winifred," she said, "you own the whole town square."

"No—just a quarter of it." I winked.

She laughed.

Thad slapped at a bug on his leg. "Did Mr. Burns find out anything new about the treasure when he went to Atlanta?"

"The Spanish government is loaning it for display to the Georgia History Museum." I jumped off Evrol and faced them. "And get this, the guy in charge of publicity for the museum is bringing a news crew down here next week. He wants to interview all of us. We're going to be on TV!"

"Sweet!" Clemmie and Thad high-fived.

Deputy Oringderff pulled up alongside Evrol and climbed out of her cruiser. "Evening, y'all. Grady, do you recognize this?" She showed me a photo.

"That's Mama's sampler that I switched for the treasure map!"

"That's what I figured, but I needed to verify," she said.

"Where did you find it? Can we have it back?"

"We found it at Muggie's house. It's evidence, so you won't get it back right away."

"What will happen to Muggie?"

"She's going to jail for a long time. She's charged with burglary, manslaughter, false imprisonment, and child endangerment for a start. And she confessed to everything. The mayor's pretty devastated about it." She nodded toward the church. "Your dad's somewhere in there, I assume."

"Yes, ma'am."

She started to walk away and then stopped. "You should know when she learned about the fire, she was horrified. She didn't mean to put your life in danger."

We watched her go into the church, then Thad said, "Speaking of samplers, what are you going to do with Elizabeth's now that it's no longer hiding in an ammo box in Clemmie's closet?"

"Dad now thinks it's an awesome family heirloom and he wants it properly preserved. It'll go on display alongside the cross at the Georgia History Museum for a while. But eventually we'll hang it in our house."

Clemmie bit her lip nervously. "Which will be...where?"

"Dad spoke to Teta Lynne. We're buying Eudora's place. He wants—"

"Yay, you're not moving away!" Clemmie threw her arms around me. Her braids swung around and smacked the back of my head. "I can't believe you didn't tell me first thing!"

"I was waiting for the right time. Dad wants to restore it and—"

Thad gasped. "Restore it! Can I help? Gothic Revival Victorians are my favorite."

"Man, that place is *enormous*," Clemmie said. "What are y'all going to do with all that space?"

"Dad wants to build furniture—rocking chairs are his specialty. Like the one he made Mama years ago. He says we'll live upstairs and have the furniture store downstairs."

"What a great idea," Clemmie said. She hopped down. "Well now that I know you're staying, I'm going to celebrate with a big old piece of Ida Rose's chocolate cake."

Thad perked right up. "Count me in." Evrol shook as he jumped off the tailgate.

"Dad's going to name the store Eudora's," I said. "So, she'll always be remembered."

"Eudora's?" Clemmie asked. "Not Eudora's Furniture or Eudora's *something*?"

I shook my head. "He likes the sound of just her name."

"But the word 'furniture' won't be on the sign," Clemmie said. "That makes no sense."

Thad stared at her. "Do you have to argue about everything?"

"I don't argue about *everything*," she scoffed.

They headed toward the church, quarreling as they went. Different as they could be, but totally good.

Just like I knew Dad and I would be.

My mockingbird had been quiet the last couple of days, and every once in a while, I could swear I heard a little canary singing.

My feathers were growing.

And my hope soared.

WAS THE WAR OF JENKINS'S EAR REALLY ABOUT AN EAR?

DESPITE ITS NAME, THE War of Jenkins's Ear was not fought because Robert Jenkins, a British sea captain, had his ear cut off by the Spanish. The relationship between Spain and England was tense long before Jenkins's hearing was reduced by half. However, the "War of Land Claims, Piracy, and Irreconcilable Trading Differences between Two Nations" doesn't sound nearly as intriguing and takes way more time to say.

So what was the War of Jenkins's Ear really about?

During the 1700s, the Caribbean Sea was a trading hot spot for the colonial powers of Spain and Great Britain. Rice, indigo, molasses, rum, and sugar meant big bucks back home in Europe. A good chunk of the Caribbean and Florida had been claimed by Spain, while Great Britain settled its New England colonies, all the way down to South Carolina. The area we now call Georgia was still up for grabs, so to speak. Sadly, neither side recognized that the lands they were claiming to be theirs were already populated by indigenous peoples.

A treaty between the two countries gave Britain the right to do *limited* trading of Caribbean goods. A few years later, following a new treaty, Britain gave Spain the right to inspect its ships to make sure they were honoring the agreement. In accordance with the agreement, Spanish coast guards began boarding and seizing ships, believing the British were smuggling contraband goods.

Let's go back to April 9, 1731, when Captain Jenkins's ship, the *Rebecca*, sat off the coast of Cuba. The *Rebecca*'s cargo was Jamaican sugar. But before she could sail for London, the Spanish boarded her for inspection. Finding the Jamaican sugar and suspecting it to be contraband, the commander, Captain Juan León Fandiño, took the sugar, and, in furious retribution, sliced off Jenkins's ear as punishment, saying, "Go, and tell your king that I will do the same if he dares to do the same."

The Spanish did not deny depriving Jenkins of his left ear, and they said he had it coming! They painted him as a smuggler and a pirate, and they weren't wrong. Even English accounts recognized that Jenkins was a well-known smuggler. In this case, two wrongs did make a right, because a right ear was all Jenkins had remaining after *that* incident.

Now, here's where it gets weird.

Captain Jenkins *saved* his severed ear. That's right, he had it pickled and kept it in a jar, and every once in a while, he'd bust it out and tell the story of the great injustice done to him by the Spanish.

Then, a year later in 1732, the British claimed Georgia. The sole purpose was to establish a protective barrier between Florida and the South Carolina colony. The relationship between Spain and England deteriorated even more. Why? Because Spain considered the Georgia colony a threat to Spanish-owned Florida and the trade routes associated with it.

By this time, word got around that Captain Jenkins still had his ear souvenir. British politicians, along with certain members of the South Sea Company took advantage of that fact. They spread the idea that if Great Britain went to war with Spain and won, Britain would have a more successful trading industry and become wealthier. They used Jenkins's ear to stir up outrage in Parliament. They demanded King George II go to war.

The king tried diplomatic means, but to no avail, and the War of Jenkins's Ear eventually broke out in 1739.

While much of the war was fought on the seas, skirmishes and even some large-scale battles took place on land. In fact, James Oglethorpe, the founder of the Georgia colony, led a botched invasion of Florida, attacking Fort St. Augustine in 1740.

However, a couple years later, he successfully defended Fort Frederica from the Spanish on St. Simons Island, Georgia.

Over time, the War of Jenkins's Ear merged into the War of Austrian Succession and eventually ended in 1748. The Georgia colony served its purpose in protecting South Carolina from Spanish threats. For the colonists, the war was a serious struggle for survival even though it had a silly name.

FOR FURTHER READING

Arndt, Gary. "The War of Jenkins' Ear." *Everything Everywhere,* podcast. https://everything-everywhere.com/the-war-of-jenkins-ear/

Britannica, T. Editors of Encyclopaedia. "War of Jenkins' Ear." Encyclopedia Britannica, August 1, 2014. https://www .britannica.com/event/War-of-Jenkins-Ear

Graboyes, Evan, and Timothy Hullar. "The War of Jenkins' Ear." *Otology & Neurotology,* February 2013. https://www.ncbi .nlm.nih.gov/pmc/articles/PMC3711623/

McConnell, Kelsey. "A Shocking Incident Led to the War of Jenkins' Ear." *The Archive,* August 26, 2021. https://explore thearchive.com/war-of-jenkins-ear

Sweet, Julie. "War of Jenkins' Ear." *New Georgia Encyclopedia,* last modified Dec 10, 2019. https://www.georgiaencyclopedia .org/articles/history-archaeology/war-of-jenkins-ear/

Towles, Louis. "War of Jenkins' Ear." *Encyclopedia of North Carolina*, January 1, 2006. https://www.ncpedia.org/jenkins-ear-war

Traynor, Robert. "The War of Jenkins' Ear." Hearing Health Matters, May 4, 2015. https://hearinghealthmatters.org /hearinginternational/2015/the-war-of-jenkins-ear/

Yadav, Alok. "War of Jenkins' Ear (1739–48)" in Historical Outline of Restoration and 18th-Century British Literature (chronology for students at George Mason University), last modified August 11, 2020. https://mason.gmu.edu/~ayadav /historical%20outline/overview.htm#top

ACKNOWLEDGMENTS

There are so many people who helped with this project. My husband David and my three children, Elenna, Jireh, and Nathan: thank you for being patient and understanding about my writing and for getting accustomed to poorly cooked dinners thrown together at the last-minute. Hey, no one got food poisoning, right?

I am very grateful for the assistance of my uber-accomplished cousin, composer Josh Gottry, for helping with musical guidance when it came to figuring out what on earth *timbre* was and how to use it in a sentence!

Thank you from across the pond to Nicola Parkman, a brilliant Brit who provided information on sampler motifs and their meanings.

Leslie Devooght and Ranger Jill Leverett—thank you both so much for telling me about tabby stone and answering *all* my questions about colonial concrete. Who knew it was so fascinating?

Thank you, Kristin Rogers for meeting with me for coffee and talking about the War of Jenkins's Ear. I truly appreciate all the time you put into that interview.

A special thank-you to my amazing, fantastically talented fellow Inkstigators: Amy Paulshock, Jan Eldredge, Leslie Santamaria, Marcea Ustler, Ruth Owens, and Charlotte Hunter. Y'all make me a better writer!

Thank you, Word Weavers for your critiques and insights.

Sally Apokedak—as always, you make sure I don't fall flat on my face when it comes to writing. Thank you for your steady and constant support and for being the best literary agent out there.

ABOUT THE AUTHOR

Taryn Souders graduated from the University of North Texas with a specialization in mathematics. She is the author of Edgar-nominated *Coop Knows the Scoop* as well as *How to (Almost) Ruin Your Summer*. She lives in Sorrento, Florida, with her family. Visit her at **tarynsouders.com**.